"We have to keep it professional," she whispered, her tone hardly convincing.

Darryl whispered into her ear. "If you say so," he said, just before sliding his tongue along the edge and sucking Camryn's earlobe between his lips.

Camryn gasped loudly, shivering with expectation. "Ohh! Darryl, you have to stop!"

Heaving a deep sigh, Darryl suddenly tapped her lightly against the curve of her hip. "I'm sorry. We should be going," he said, as he gently separated himself from her and stood up. "Before I do something we'll both regret."

Moving to her feet, Camryn wrapped her arms tightly around her torso. She took a deep breath, closing her eyes briefly as she struggled to regain her composure. The man had her feeling some kind of way and it was almost too much. She lifted her face to the bright sun, allowing the heated rays to tenderly soothe the unrest brewing inside of her. When she finally opened her eyes, Darryl was staring at her, a pained expression wrinkling his brow. He reached a large hand out to gently stroke the side of her face. Without him saying a word, Camryn felt that she could feel exactly what he was feeling. She took a step toward him, moving her body easily against his.

The look she gave him was enchanting, her stare an overflowing fountain of emotion. "I won't regret it," she whispered as she slid her arms around his waist, the soft curves of her body pressing tightly to the hard lines of his. "I won't have any regrets at all," she repeated.

Books by Deborah Fletcher Melloy

Harlequin Kimani Romance

DEBORAH FLETCHER MELLO

Writing since forever, Deborah Fletcher Mello can't imagine herself doing anything else. Her first romance novel, *Take Me to Heart,* earned her a 2004 Romance Slam Jam nomination for "Best New Author." In 2005 she received "Book of the Year" and "Favorite Heroine" nominations for her novel *The Right Side of Love,* and in 2009 won a *RT Book Reviews* "Reviewer's Choice Award" for *Tame a Wild Stallion.* Deborah's eleventh novel, *Promises to a Stallion,* earned her a 2011 Romance Slam Jam nomination for "Hero of the Year."

For Deborah, writing is as necessary as breathing and she firmly believes that if she could not write she would cease to exist. For Deborah, the ultimate thrill is to weave a story that leaves her audience feeling full, and complete, as if they've just enjoyed an incredible meal. Born and raised in Connecticut, Deborah now maintains base camp in North Carolina but considers home to be wherever the moment moves her.

Truly Yours

DEBORAH
FLETCHER
MELLO

HARLEQUIN® KIMANI™ ROMANCE

To Priscilla Meza Mello
May your journey be everything you want it to be
…And more!

Recycling programs
for this product may
not exist in your area.

ISBN-13: 978-0-373-86317-4

TRULY YOURS

Copyright © 2013 by Deborah Fletcher Mello

For questions and comments about the quality of this book please contact us
at CustomerService@Harlequin.com.

Printed in U.S.A.

Dear Reader,

Allow me to express my sincerest appreciation for all the support and love you all have shown me. I am extremely grateful for each book you've purchased, each comment you've shared, every review you've written, and all the critiques that have hopefully helped me get better and better with each story.

I hope you are starting to love my Boudreaux family as much as I do. Breathing life into Darryl and Camryn's story was not without some challenges but I hope you'll agree it was well worth the ride. Admittedly, Darryl Boudreaux put me through some changes. If it wasn't for Camryn Charles, I probably would have pulled my hair out! Camryn is definitely the yin to his yang!

I do love hearing what you think, so please don't hesitate to contact me at DeborahMello@aol.com.

Until the next time, take care and God bless.

With much love,

Deborah Fletcher Mello

www.deborahmello.blogspot.com

Chapter 1

Annoyance painted Darryl Boudreaux's expression as his gaze shifted from the line of police cars encroaching in his driveway to the Jaguar XF pulling into it. He prepared himself for the barrage of questions he knew would be coming from his older sister, Maitlyn Parks, who was flinging her thin frame out of the luxury vehicle.

Minutes earlier Darryl had been unnerved by the sound of sirens blaring toward the front of his home as his former girlfriend Asia Landry laid sobbing into the wool fibers of his newly installed carpet. The small-caliber handgun that she'd pointed in his direction moments before lay on the floor by her side, still as ominous as when it had been aimed at his head. Now he stood, troubled by the spectacle of it all, just imagining what his neighbors had to be thinking. He let out a deep sigh, blowing warm air past his full lips.

"What the hell is going on here?" Maitlyn asked as she bounded up his front steps. "Are you all right?"

"Fine as wine," he said sarcastically, his expression shifting into a mask of indifference. "What makes you think anything could be wrong?"

Maitlyn shot him a look of irritation, countering with her own sarcasm. "Uh, maybe because Asia has her face pressed against the glass in the back of that police car, looking like she stepped right out of someone's horror movie, that's why!" Maitlyn pointed with her index finger.

Darryl sighed. "She had to have one last hurrah."

"Darryl, this is—" Maitlyn started before the two were interrupted by a uniformed police officer. The man extended a clipboard in Darryl's direction.

"Mr. Boudreaux, sir, we just need to get your signature. Then we're going to take Miss Landry down to the police station."

"What will happen then?" Darryl asked as he took the clipboard from the man's hand and swiped his moniker across the document that was secured to it.

"Miss Landry will be booked and held until she can see a judge in the morning. He and the district attorney will decide what happens then, sir. I can assure you, though, that they take possession of a weapon and threat to cause bodily harm very seriously."

Darryl nodded as he handed the formal complaint back to the officer. "I leave for New Orleans later tonight. I'm scheduled to be away on business for the next few months. Is that going to be a problem?"

The officer shook his head. "I don't think so, sir.

And we have a number to contact you should it be necessary, correct?"

"Yes, and thank you. I'll also make sure my attorney contacts the D.A.'s office about that restraining order."

As the man in uniform wished him and Maitlyn a good night, Darryl pushed his hands deep into the pockets of his khakis. His gazed locked on the woman whose face appeared permanently fused to the faintly tinted glass pane.

Asia Landry looked crazed, but not nearly as crazed as when Darryl had told her their relationship was finished and he no longer had the desire for a future with her. He had tried to be as civil as possible, hoping against all odds that they could end their relationship amicably and remain friends. But when he had said goodbye and had wished her a bright and prosperous future, the one good screw in her brain stem had come unhinged.

As Darryl and his sister watched the police cars pull out of his driveway, he couldn't help but wish that he'd listened to his brothers when they told him to break up with Asia on neutral territory, their suggestions ranging from a local Starbucks to the public library. But no, he'd wanted to be more sensitive to Asia's feelings, not wanting to cause her any public embarrassment, and so he'd invited her to his home.

Now, as his neighbors waved at him, eyeing him with raised brows before disappearing behind their own closed doors, he was the one left feeling mortified. Maitlyn's nagging suddenly broke through, intruding on his moment of reflection.

"We told you she was crazy! How many times did

we tell you that witch was a raving lunatic!" Maitlyn sighed with exasperation.

"Thank you, Mattie. Smack my hand for not paying any attention to all that advice you and the rest of our family dish out every minute of every day," Darryl said dryly.

Maitlyn cut an eye in his direction as she assessed the wreckage in his living room. His glass coffee table had been shattered. His personal possessions had been thrown from one side of the room to the other. Everything was in a complete state of disarray. And then she saw the bullet holes through the family portrait that hung on the wall. Maitlyn's palm flew to her mouth as she stepped in to take a closer look. Tears rose to her eyes.

She shook her head as she turned to face her brother, meeting his intense stare. Noting her distress, he shrugged his shoulders as he reached to wrap his arms around her. "It's okay, Maitlyn," he said, trying to make light of the situation.

"No, it's not," she said, visibly shaking. "You could have been hurt. She could have killed you!"

As Darryl hugged his sister tightly, he had no words. He could still hear the harsh sound of that gun being cocked and the shots that had rung through the air as bullets had whizzed by his head. He refused to let it show but the moment had been life-altering, everything feeling as if it had changed. He closed his eyes as he gathered his thoughts.

"I'm fine and that's all that matters. Now, if you help me get this mess cleaned up, I'll buy you dinner."

Maitlyn swiped at her eyes. "Don't worry about

cleaning up. I'll handle it while you're gone. Are you all packed?"

He nodded. "Yeah, my luggage is in the bedroom."

"Then let's just go grab something to eat and I'll make sure everything is as good as new after I drop you off at the airport. Right now, though, I need a drink."

"Are you sure?" Darryl questioned.

"What's a big sister for?" Maitlyn said, forcing a smile on her face.

Darryl smiled with her. "Well, since you're being a good big sister, I need one more thing from you," he stated firmly.

"What's that?"

"I need you to promise me you won't tell the folks about what happened."

"Darryl!"

"Promise me, Mattie!"

Maitlyn met her brother's gaze and held it for a brief moment. As she slowly nodded her head, she slid both her hands behind her back and crossed her fingers. "Whatever you want, Darryl," she said unconvincingly.

"I mean it," Darryl intoned as he headed toward the back bedroom and his luggage, instinctively knowing that every one of his siblings would know about what happened before the clock struck midnight. "Don't you dare tell Mommy and Daddy!"

Grabbing his leather bags, he headed back to the front of his home and his sister, who was still assessing the damage Asia had caused. As he stood beside her, he was suddenly grateful for the time away. By midnight he'd be on the red-eye flight headed east, soaring sky-high as he headed to his parents' home in New Orleans.

Tomorrow he'd be back to work, ready for one of the most rewarding opportunities of his career. And with any luck everything about his time with Asia Landry would soon be nothing but a bad memory.

Katherine Boudreaux tossed up her hands in exasperation. "She tried to kill you? Lord, have mercy!" she exclaimed, the palm of her hand pressed tight to her chest.

"Asia did not try to kill me, Mom," Darryl said as he looked toward his brother for help.

The oldest of the Boudreaux offspring, Mason Boudreaux, shrugged his shoulders. "Don't look at me. I wasn't there. I was just repeating what Maitlyn told me."

Darryl blew out a deep sigh. He opened his mouth to make his point when their father interjected. "Just for the record, son, when a woman points a gun at you and pulls the trigger, she's past the point of trying to scare you," Senior Boudreaux said matter-of-factly.

Darryl rolled his eyes. "Maitlyn has blown this whole thing out of proportion."

"We wouldn't have even known if it hadn't been for your sister," Katherine noted, her finger waving at her son. "And I'm not happy about that. I'm not happy at all." Katherine shook her head. "Come get some breakfast. Y'all got a long day today," she ordered.

Mason glanced at his brother. Both men knew their mother was angry and Katherine Boudreaux angry could get them all hurt. He tipped his head toward Darryl as he turned to follow their mother.

Darryl muttered under his breath as he made his way

out of the room. "I swear I'm going to wring Maitlyn's neck for this."

Mason smiled as he and his father locked gazes. "I'll talk to him," he said softly.

Senior nodded his approval. "Darryl needs to take this more seriously. Now, let's go get some breakfast before your mother beats him, you and me, too."

By the time Darryl and Mason made their way through New Orleans to the Roosevelt Hotel, the two men were laughing heartily. Breakfast had been tense as their mother had slapped bacon, eggs and grits onto their porcelain plates. But by the end of the meal she'd calmed down enough to listen to Darryl's apology. Mason had been poking fun at him since.

"It's just like what happened when that mess went down with me in Thailand. The old folks were mad because they heard about it from the girls and not from me. Your sisters will get you in trouble every time. I don't know why you haven't learned that yet," Mason said with a robust chuckle.

Darryl shook his head. "Maitlyn better be glad we're not kids anymore, because I'd find a mud hole for her sure 'nuff!"

Mason grinned. "But Maitlyn kept her promise. She didn't tell them. She just told the rest of us. Your other sisters all called and broke the news to them. Then, of course, the minute I walked through the door they were looking at me to confirm it. You know you should have called each one of us and made us pinkie swear."

"I'm still going to wring her neck," Darryl exclaimed.

Mason shook his head. "So what do you plan to do?"

His brother shrugged. "Nothing. The court system will deal with Asia and I plan to focus all my attention on this project."

"I'm sure that throwing yourself into your work will make it all go away," he said, a hint of sarcasm in his tone.

With a roll of his eyes, Darryl changed the subject. "So, what's Mr. Charles like? I'm really looking forward to working with him and his firm."

Mason smiled. "Kenneth is quite the character. I think this will be a great partnership."

"I'm anxious to meet him and his son, Cam. That's his son's name, right, Cam Charles? I admire a lot of his work, as well."

Mason's eyes widened. "Oh, Cam's not a—" he started, suddenly interrupted by the cell phone chiming loudly from the breast pocket of his suit jacket. He held up his index finger, gesturing for Darryl to hold his thought. Mason pulled the device into his hand, grinning as the smartphone's screen projected an image of his wife.

"Hey, baby!"

Phaedra Stallion-Boudreaux exclaimed joyously on the other end. "Good morning, good-lookin'! Are you busy?"

"Darryl and I are headed into a meeting. Are you okay?"

"I'm fine. Missing you, though."

"I miss you, too, darling," he said, his voice dropping an octave. "How long are you planning to stay in Texas?"

"That's why I'm calling you, actually. I have to fly to

New York. I've been hired to get some shots of the city for a tourism project. I'll be there for at least a week, and then I'll head to New Orleans."

Mason nodded into the receiver. His wife's photography career was important to her and despite the abundance of wealth they shared, he supported her desire to work and have her own. She'd been fiercely independent when they'd first met and was even more so since she'd become his wife.

"Mason, you still there?" Phaedra questioned.

"Sorry, baby. I'm fine," he responded. "Are you going to be okay traveling by yourself?" he asked.

Phaedra laughed. "I can't believe you asked me that," she said. "But for the record, I won't be alone. Mark is going with me."

Mason laughed with her. "You know how I worry about you."

"I'm not the one who goes around getting kidnapped," she teased, reminding him of the time she'd had to call upon her newly discovered brothers to help find him in Thailand. She continued, "I'll be fine. You're just as bad as my brothers."

Her husband grinned as he thought about his new in-laws. Phaedra had only recently come to know her four brothers, John, Matthew, Mark and Luke Stallion. Doing business with the family had been the catalyst that had opened the doors to his relationship with their baby sister. He would be forever grateful. "We'll, I'm glad he'll be there with you. Just stay in touch with me, please."

"You know I will," she said, making kissing noises through the receiver. "I love you!"

Mason laughed softly. "I love you, too, baby! I'll call you after my meeting, okay?"

"I can't wait," Phaedra said.

Disconnecting the call, Mason stood with a wide grin on his face. He tossed a glance over at Darryl, who was rolling his dark eyes. "Live and learn, Darryl. My woman never tried to shoot me," he said smugly.

"Asia wasn't my woman," Darryl said sarcastically.

Their bantering continued as they made their way to the upper suites that Mason had rented for temporary office space. As they stepped over the threshold, the doors closing behind them, both men shifted headfirst into business mode.

Chapter 2

"Boudreaux Towers is a multilevel office complex the likes of which has never been seen in New Orleans, Louisiana." The comment came from Kenneth Charles, renowned architect and owner of the design firm Charles & Charles Architecture. "This will be a magnificent partnership for us." He and his daughter were riding in the company limo to their meeting. He lifted his gaze from the iPad he was making notes on to stare in her direction.

Camryn Charles eyed her father back. "And we'll be working directly with Mason?" she asked.

Her father nodded. "I don't know if you're aware or not but he sold off his hotel business. This is a new venture for him and I'm honored that he wants us to design the building. He has a brother that will be working on this project, as well. I haven't had the opportunity to meet him yet." Kenneth paused as he leaned forward in his seat, passing a prospectus to his daughter. "And this is going to be a great opportunity for you, as well, Camryn. I've given it a lot of thought and I want you to take the lead on this project. Mason and I have agreed that you should head the design team."

Camryn's eyes widened as she took the documents from her father's hand. "Really?"

The man's salt-and-pepper head moved up and down. "You're making a solid name for yourself in the industry, independent of me and the business. It's been impressive, and I think if you design the newest skyscraper in downtown New Orleans, it will take both you and the business to a whole new level."

The young woman smiled warmly. "I appreciate the confidence, Father," she said, flipping through the documents in her lap.

Camryn fought to contain the excitement that sizzled in the pit of her stomach. Although she'd been eager to work on a new project with her father, to have him hand her the reins of one of the company's biggest contracts was a big deal for the both of them. Determined to prove herself worthy of his trust, Camryn couldn't wait to get started.

As their driver stopped the car in front of the Roosevelt Hotel and moved to open the door for them, she turned to her father. "How much creative control do I have?" she asked.

The man eyed her teasingly. "How much do you want?"

She grinned. "Why doesn't that sound promising, Father?"

He chuckled warmly. "As far as I'm concerned, Camryn, you have full and total creative control. However," he concluded, tossing her a wink of his eye, "you'll have to negotiate the specifics of that with our client."

"I hope our client is an old softy like you, then!"

Her father laughed. "There's nothing soft about your old man, Camryn Charles. Not one single thing."

Camryn laughed with him. "So there's hope for Mr. Boudreaux, is that what you're saying?"

Kenneth grinned. "For some reason, I think the Boudreaux family is in for more than they bargained for."

The two men sat at the large conference table as Mason detailed the budget for his new multimillion-dollar building. Darryl listened intently, digesting the details like a good meal. He'd been inundated with information since he arrived, his brother's excitement fueling his own. Adding to that exhilaration was discovering that Mason had hired Kenneth Charles to work on the architectural design.

Kenneth Charles was one of his idols, having won numerous awards for his work. He was considered an architectural genius amongst his peers, and Darryl was excited about the prospect of working with the legend. His thoughts were interrupted by a knock on the conference room door, the entrance swinging open easily.

Both Darryl and Mason came to their feet as Kenneth Charles made an entrance. "Mason, how are you?" the man said, extending a large hand as the two old friends greeted each other warmly.

"It's good to see you, Kenneth." He gestured behind him. "Let me introduce you to my brother. Darryl Boudreaux, this is Kenneth Charles. Kenneth, my brother Darryl."

"It's an honor to meet you, sir," Darryl said, his eyes wide with awe.

"Your brother speaks quite highly of you, Darryl. I understand from Mason that you are quite talented in your own right. Is that true, son?" Kenneth asked.

Darryl shrugged ever so slightly. "I think my brother is a bit biased, sir."

"Family usually is. Trust me when I tell you that the work I've done isn't all that impressive, either. However, to hear my daughter tell it, you'd think I'd built stairwells past the moon and straight to heaven."

A soft voice echoed from the entrance behind them. "Actually, Father, I tell people you've built stairwells past heaven and into the stratosphere."

Darryl turned toward the entrance and stared. There was no missing the familial resemblance between Mr. Charles and the young woman entering the room. Without realizing it, Darryl found himself holding his breath. The stunning beauty had commanded his full and undivided attention.

She shared her father's warm chocolate complexion and large dark eyes. He assumed that the full lips and pouty mouth that begged to be kissed had been inherited from her mother. In the tailored navy skirt and ruffled white blouse she wore, there was no denying the woman had a figure that could make even a strong man beg for her attention. She was curvaceous with a full bustline, whisper-thin waist and pleasingly thick hips. As he stared, Darryl suddenly felt weak, his legs feeling like jelly. He had to fight to shake the unnerving sensation. He took a deep breath and held it.

Mason laughed. "That's right! Give credit where credit is due!" he said as he moved to wrap the young woman in a quick hug. "How are you, Camryn? It's good to see you again."

"I'm doing very well, Mason. It's good to see you again, too. And congratulations! Father tells me you recently got married!"

"Yes, I did." Mason grinned. "I hope to introduce you and your father to Phaedra in the very near future."

The young woman smiled sweetly. "I can't wait to meet her. It looks like marriage is serving you well."

"It definitely is!" Mason said, nodding his agreement.

"Camryn, come say hello," her father interrupted. "Darryl, this is my daughter, Camryn. Cam, this is Mason's brother Darryl Boudreaux."

The young woman tilted her head in greeting. There was no missing the good-looking man who'd caught her eye when she'd entered the room. Darryl Boudreaux was quite the male specimen. Standing tall and lean in a black silk suit, white shirt and red necktie, he had distinctive features that hinted at an African-Asian ancestry. He boasted slightly angular eyes, a thin nose, a high cheek line and full, pillow-soft lips. His complexion was a rich, deep umber and Camryn felt her heart quicken a beat or two as she met his intense gaze. "Mr. Boudreaux, it's my pleasure."

Still in awe, Darryl stared, his eyes wide, his mouth agape. "You're *Cam* Charles?" he questioned as he took her extended hand, her palm gliding like silk against his.

The beautiful woman laughed lightly. "Is that a problem?"

Darryl shook his head, cutting an eye in Mason's direction. "No, I just wasn't expecting—"

Mason laughed heartily as he interrupted. "Sorry about that. I think my brother thought you were a man."

Camryn nodded ever so slightly. "That happens often, but I'm very much a woman," she said with a soft chuckle that made Darryl smile. She pulled her hand from his, acutely aware of the hold he had on her fingers. The two were still studying each other intently.

Darryl finally shook the daze that had consumed him. "It's a pleasure to meet you, Ms. Charles," he said.

"Please, call me Camryn," she said, "or Cam."

Darryl nodded as he pulled a chair out for Camryn and gestured for her father to take a seat. He caught his brother's eye and nodded. "Shall we get down to business?"

Hours later, Darryl pulled at the necktie around his neck. Like his brother and Kenneth Charles, he'd tossed his suit jacket aside some time ago. The back-and-forth banter between the two companies was beginning to take its toll on all of them.

"I don't agree," Darryl was saying. "You have to keep the safety factor first and foremost in the design."

"I'm fully aware of that," Camryn responded, clearly perturbed by his insinuations. "However, the aesthetic value of the building and how it will complement the landscape is equally as important."

Darryl shrugged his broad shoulders as he tossed his

ink pen to the tabletop. He took a deep breath, totally annoyed that Camryn Charles was challenging him.

"I'm sorry, but what actually will your role be in this project?" Camryn suddenly asked. She was staring directly at Darryl, the two having already butted heads over more than that one issue.

Standing, Darryl leaned over the table, his weight resting on his arms. "Pro-ject man-a-ger," he replied, uttering each syllable distinctly. "It's my responsibility to see that this project comes in well within budget, to our exact specifications. I will be accountable for every single detail, including the specifics of the final design."

Camryn rolled her eyes. It hadn't taken long for her to realize that Darryl Boudreaux was going to be a royal pain in her well-rounded behind. The man had criticized, critiqued and questioned every suggestion and comment that she'd had. With the way he'd been hammering her, you would have thought that she'd had no previous experience in the design and building industry. Clearly, the man didn't have a clue and she didn't appreciate him being so confrontational. She also didn't have a problem letting him know how she felt.

Camryn came to her feet, as well, crossing her arms over her chest as she met his gaze evenly. Annoyance tapped the toe of her leather pump. "And tell me again what makes you *qualified* for the job, because from my perspective our firm is more than capable of meeting your brother's wish list without outside supervision."

Darryl bristled. "Perhaps, but my brother would be unwise to not have a system of checks and balances. You don't build a multimillion-dollar office complex by putting all your eggs in one basket. And as far as my qualifications go, I have a Ph.D. in mechanical engineering and I'm a licensed building contractor. My forte is my penchant for details. *All* aspects of the details. So I am more than capable of overseeing this project *and* you."

Both Mason and Kenneth leaned back in their seats, obviously amused by the standoff. Mason chuckled softly. "I think this is a good time to call it a day," he said calmly. He cut his eye toward Kenneth. "We can pick this back up tomorrow, same time."

Kenneth nodded. "I agree. But I'm also thinking that it would probably be a very good idea for Camryn and Darryl to get to know each other better, especially since they're going to be working so closely together." He picked up his iPad and typed into the keypad. "Do you eat seafood, Darryl?" he inquired. His gaze never left his device. "And sit down, Camryn!" Kenneth commanded.

"Yes, sir," Darryl answered, still squared off against the man's daughter.

Camryn huffed as she finally dropped back into her seat. Darryl followed, each still eyeing the other warily.

Kenneth continued. "Camryn loves seafood. My secretary will make reservations for you two for dinner. You don't have anything planned, do you, Darryl?" he said, finally lifting his eyes to look at the young man.

Mason interjected. "No, sir. Darryl has no plans whatsoever. He's here to work, no matter what that might entail. Isn't that right, Darryl?" he said, answering on his brother's behalf.

"Good," Kenneth said, nodding his head. "Camryn is free, as well."

"Father!"

He ignored his daughter's treaty, dropping his gaze back to his electronic device. "You two kids have seven o'clock dinner reservations at The Bourbon House. Take the time to ask whatever you need to ask each other so that we can finalize the details of this project when we meet tomorrow. Is that clear, Cam?" he said firmly.

"Yes, sir," she said through gritted teeth.

Mason smiled. "You, too, little brother," he said, tossing Darryl a quick wink. "Work it out!"

Darryl's eyes narrowed into thin slits as he shot his brother a look. Mason seemed to be enjoying the discomfort he was causing him, a glint of mischief shimmering in the look he threw back. Biting his tongue, Darryl glanced over at Camryn. She was looking at him closely. As he nodded his head, he couldn't help but think that working it out might be a whole lot easier if the woman wasn't so damn intoxicating.

Chapter 3

Darryl was still heated when he and Mason arrived back at their family home. His brother had found the whole situation amusing, which had irritated him even more. He was grateful that neither of his parents was home, just imagining the feedback that would have come if Mason had had the opportunity to fill them in on what had happened between him and that woman.

Camryn Charles had worked his nerves and having her father and his brother manipulating the situation didn't help. He slammed his bedroom door closed and threw his body across the twin bed. He was further irritated that he now had to spend the evening with her, because after his experience with Asia, spending the evening with any woman was not high on his priority list.

From start to finish Asia Landry had made life difficult at best, their entire relationship being one firestorm after another. Jealousy fueled Asia's spirit more times than not. The first time Darryl had been introduced to the green-eyed monster, she'd keyed his car, leaving the vehicle looking like an Etch A Sketch gone horribly wrong. Apparently being too friendly with a sales clerk had been his crime. He should have cut his ties with Asia then but after her tearful apology he'd welcomed her back into his arms.

Asia hacking his personal email "to confirm that he was cheating" had been the last straw. Her threatening his life had cemented his conviction. He was done and finished. Darryl refused to be with a woman who clearly didn't trust him. And he refused to be with a woman he couldn't trust to deal with her frustrations and anger as though she had some God-given sense. Thinking about everything he'd gone through with Asia tightened a knot in the pit of his stomach. Asia had burned him. Bad. And now, thanks to Asia, Darryl was adamant that no other woman would stand an ice cube's chance of getting under his skin. Not even one as enticing as Camryn Charles.

Camryn arrived early for her dinner with Darryl Boudreaux. She'd contemplated not showing at all but had figured a few uncomfortable hours with Darryl was far better than dealing with her father's wrath at their meeting tomorrow. She allowed the restaurant's hostess to guide her to their reserved table.

As she settled down into her seat, she was suddenly nervous about their dinner. There was something about Darryl Boudreaux that she found equally irritating and intriguing. Good looks aside, the man's confidence bor-

dered on arrogance. Clearly, his engineering skills and
construction background made him an ideal partner for
the project. But he had a serious control problem and
she had an issue with him questioning her abilities. He
was obviously going to be problematic and Camryn
hadn't expected to work quite so hard.

She took a quick sip of water from the crystal glass
that rested on the table in front of her. Glancing around
the restaurant, she couldn't help but notice the many
couples who were more intent on each other than on
their meals. Camryn suddenly couldn't remember the
last time she and a man had sat together so totally and
completely focused on each other.

She saw Darryl before he saw her. As he eased into
the restaurant, he paused to take in his surroundings.
It was evident from the expression on his face that he
had about as much desire to be there as she did. For a
brief moment it looked as if he might turn tail and run
but he didn't. Instead he appeared to search her out
with his eyes.

He had beautiful eyes, Camryn thought. She hated
admitting that his dark, seductive orbs made her weak
in the knees. If she was honest, being in his presence
was like walking through fire. He made heat radiate
out of every one of her pores until she was completely
drained. But there was also something soft-spoken and
gentle about his spirit, like a welcome, cool sweet breeze
even when he was being a thorn in her right cheek. But
it remained to be seen if they could come to an understanding and work together in harmony. Her full lips
lifted to a warm smile as he finally approached the
table, his own expression softening considerably.

Darryl was suddenly unnerved by the eagerness that consumed him as he sauntered slowly to where Camryn was sitting. The attractive woman was even more stunning, having changed from her business attire to a form-fitting Herve Leger dress. The fabric's vibrant red color complemented her complexion nicely. Her dark brown curls had been slicked back into a neat ponytail, and big bold earrings decorated her earlobes. Her makeup was impeccable and her easy smile showed dazzling white teeth. Her dark eyes were large and bright, her crystal complexion reminding him of deep, rich molasses. The sight of her took his breath away.

"I'm not late, am I?" Darryl asked, a quiver of heat shooting through his spirit. He tried to be casual as he pulled out the chair on the other side of the table and sat down.

Camryn took a deep breath and swallowed before speaking. "No, not at all, Darryl. I was actually a few minutes early."

Darryl's smile widened. "So, here we are," he said as a wave of nervous energy seemed to blanket the space around them.

"Here we are," Camryn echoed, suddenly feeling like a grade-schooler with her first crush.

The silence was unnerving and both were grateful when their server moved to the table to take their orders.

"Bourbon. Definitely bourbon," Camryn said, her eyebrows lifted in jest.

Camryn laughed. "I'll take mine straight," she added. "Three fingers, please!"

By the time the drinks were delivered, the two were making small talk. Camryn commented on the unusually warm weather and an unplanned shopping excursion. Darryl reflected on his flight into town and the storms that had delayed his travels. Camryn bragged about the two awards she'd recently won for the family business. Darryl detailed the multimillion-dollar project he'd worked on before being hired by his brother. She talked about her father and their family business. He shared his vision for Boudreaux Towers and what might come after. They shied away from sharing any personal information, only very briefly mentioning anything about their respective families. Neither ventured to divulge whether or not they were in a romantic relationship. Instead, the duo had seemed to come to an unspoken agreement of not wanting to know if there was someone significant in the other's personal life.

Darryl finished his drink first and over her feigned protests ordered another for each of them. His dry sense of humor made her smile and soon the laughter rang easily between them. Camryn liked how he looked into her eyes when they talked, his gaze sometimes skirting over her features as if he were trying to remember every line and dimple in her profile.

Darryl liked how she sometimes tapped his arm and hand when she laughed. The flattering gesture and soft touch both excited him and made him feel guilty.

Just before their entrée was served, Camryn excused herself to the restroom, needing a quick moment to recompose. Staring at her reflection in the polished mirror, she found herself grinning from ear to ear. She hated to admit it but she was having a really good time and that Darryl was actually likable. She giggled softly, glancing at a woman who'd entered the space behind her. The woman smiled back just before she disappeared behind a stall door. Taking a deep breath, Camryn touched up her makeup and then headed back to the table.

"Everything come out okay?" Darryl asked as she sat back down.

Camryn paused, meeting his teasing gaze. "Everything came out just fine, thank you!"

Darryl laughed heartily. "Sorry. I couldn't resist."

She laughed with him. "My brother Jason used to make the same bad joke when we were kids."

"My brothers and I still make the same bad jokes. My sisters hate it when we do that to them." He paused, a slight smile pulling at his mouth. "We do it anyway," he concluded.

Before she could reply, the waiter delivered their meals to the table, setting an appetizer of fried calamari between the two of them. Darryl had chosen the seared tuna and she compared his plate to her crabmeat-and-lobster pasta.

"It all looks good!" she said, the decadent aromas rising to her nostrils.

Darryl nodded his agreement. "It does look good but let's bless the table before we taste it, please," he said.

Camryn dropped the fork in her hand back to the tabletop and slid her hands into her lap. She stole a quick look at Darryl as he closed his eyes and lowered his head in prayer.

"Precious Lord, bless this food that we are about to receive for the nourishment of our bodies. And make us ever mindful of the needs of others. In Christ's name we pray. Amen."

"Amen," Camryn echoed, lifting her gaze to his. A burst of nervous energy fluttered in her midsection and she quickly shifted her eyes back to her plate.

"Is something wrong?" Darryl questioned as he pulled a forkful of food into his mouth.

She shook her head. "No, nothing at all," she said, not willing to admit that it had been quite some time since she'd been in the presence of a man who prayed so readily, so openly and with such ease. Her father was a praying man. She had often imagined what it might be like to be in a relationship with a man who actually walked his faith. As she pondered the possibilities, she cut an eye toward Darryl, who seemed totally focused on his meal.

She was taken aback when Darryl leaned across the table and lifted a forkful of her pasta. She watched as he slid it past his lips and chewed. "Was it good?" she asked, amused by his boldness.

Darryl nodded easily, unconcerned by his brazen behavior. "Very. So is the tuna," he said, passing a bite of his own dinner in her direction. "Here, give it a try," he cajoled. Camryn rested her hand on his as he guided the flatware toward her mouth. Heat wafted in the core of Darryl's groin as he watched her take a bite, her tongue slipping sweetly past her lips, her fingertips tapping gently against his skin. It was suddenly hot and both reached for their beverage glasses at the same time.

He chuckled softly and Camryn laughed with him. Turning back to their meals, they resumed the small talk, discussing everything and nothing. A spirited debate about politics and education was engaging, with both making valid points that gave the other something to consider.

Soon the hostess brought them dessert. Darryl hadn't anticipated the decadent layers of mousse and pastry drizzled in chocolate and topped with whipped cream. Neither was he expecting it when Camryn dipped her manicured finger into the sweet treat, drawing it through her lips to her tongue. The erotic gesture lengthened a rock-hard erection in his slacks, the thick of it pressing tight against the fabric. Darryl quickly crossed his legs, accidentally kicking the table as he did. Their dishes and utensils clattered noisily.

The ensuing silence was thundering. It dropped down over the table like an unexpected storm. Both Camryn and Darryl refocused on the food on their plates, struggling with the rise of emotion that seemed to sweep between them. Darryl was chewing so intently that he bit down on his tongue. He cursed under his breath.

"What's wrong?" Camryn asked.

His response was brusque as he threw his cloth napkin to the table and reached for his drink glass. "Nothing!"

She watched him, her eyes blinking rapidly. "And you're yelling at me because…"

"I wasn't yelling. I just…I…" Darryl stammered, his erection twitching for attention. He couldn't find the words to say he was unnerved by her presence. It felt good to be with her and he wasn't supposed to be having such a good time. She excited him and he didn't want to be excited by Camryn Charles. He lifted his eyes to stare into hers. "Look," he said finally. "We know we can get along. That should make your father and my brother very happy."

She nodded. "I'm sure it will. Let's just agree to smile and pretend we like each other until we get this job done."

"Pretend. Right." Darryl nodded. "And let's agree that you have full creative control as long as your design encompasses all of my safety recommendations. And I mean *all*."

"Agreed."

Darryl sighed and then tossed back the last of his drink. He unconsciously licked his lips, his tongue sweeping over his bottom lip before he sucked it in and bit down.

"Dinner is on my father," Camryn said as she suddenly stood tall, reaching for her clutch. "It's been a pleasure, Mr. Boudreaux."

"The pleasure has been all mine, Ms. Charles." Still conscious of the rise of nature between his legs, Darryl hesitated for a quick moment, the two staring at each other awkwardly. "May I walk you to your car?" he finally asked as he felt the problematic fullness begin to subside.

She shook her head vehemently. "No. That won't be necessary. I'll be fine."

"See you tomorrow, then," Darryl called out as Camryn turned on her high heels and scurried across the room. "Have a good night!" he chimed as she reached the front door, gave a quick wave of her hand and disappeared outside.

Camryn rushed to her car, her cheeks heated. Once she was locked inside her vehicle, she dropped her forehead down onto the steering wheel, her breath coming in heavy gasps. Her nipples pressed hard against the fabric of her dress and moisture puddled between her legs, her silk thong saturated. It had taken every ounce of fortitude she possessed not to throw herself at the good-looking Darryl Boudreaux. The moment had become so heated that all she could think about was what it might have been like to have his lips pressed against her own. Camryn hated to admit it but if Darryl had asked, she would have agreed to almost anything.

She took a deep breath and held it, counting to ten in her head. When she finally blew the air out, her nipples had receded and the quiver between her thighs was almost nonexistent. Her breathing finally steadied and she started the ignition.

As she pulled out of the parking space, she finally felt a semblance of normal. It was unfathomable to her that any man could have her quivering so unabashedly without ever laying a finger on her. Camryn shook her head at the thought. Despite having known men in her past who'd excited her sensibilities, Camryn couldn't recall any man who'd ever had the impact on her that Darryl seemed to be having.

Although everything felt out of sorts and the feelings she was currently experiencing for Darryl were completely out of her character, she knew that she could slow the momentum down and take back her control. And she was determined to take back her control. As far as she was concerned, Darryl Boudreaux would be one man who wouldn't stand a chance of ever getting the best of her.

Chapter 4

"Really, it went well!" Darryl exclaimed, annoyance punctuating his tone. He shifted his gaze toward his brother and then back down to the morning newspaper.

Mason returned the look, skepticism painting his expression. "And you two ironed out all of your differences, in one night?"

Darryl sighed deeply. "What part of 'I have it handled' don't you understand?"

Mason raised an eyebrow. "I just need to make sure we're not going to have any issues with you and Camryn. You were a little hostile yesterday."

Darryl stuck his face further into the newspaper he was pretending to read. If nothing else, he fully intended to ensure that nothing interfered with the project. He could not, however, promise that there would be no issues with Camryn Charles, because he already had issues with the beautiful woman. Issues that two ice-cold showers had still not resolved. Darryl shifted in his seat, recrossing one leg over the other.

He changed the subject. "I've arranged for Camryn and me to do a site tour this afternoon."

Mason nodded. "Good deal. And if you're sure you have everything under control, I might fly to New York tonight to surprise my wife."

Darryl smiled. "Give Phaedra a hug and kiss from me," he said sweetly.

Mason nodded. "Will do! And please, don't screw up my building before I get back."

"I won't screw up your building, Mason."

Hours later Mason and Kenneth swiped both their signatures across the final contracts, cementing the partnership between the two families. Camryn stood off to the side, an easy smile gracing her face. She fought not to steal a quick glance at Darryl. Throughout the entire meeting both had been unusually quiet and exceptionally polite with one another. And each had gone out of their way to avoid any form of contact with the other, eye or otherwise.

The previous night had incited a desire that neither had bargained for. It was consuming, like a tidal wave that had swelled thick and full, threatening everything in its wake. Neither one would admit to it but the sensation had them both reeling, unable to fathom what might happen if they didn't maintain some control.

Darryl rose to his feet, pulling his suit jacket closed. Extending his hand toward Mr. Charles, he smiled warmly. "Congratulations, sir! We look forward to working with you and your daughter," he said, tossing a nod of his head toward Camryn, who smiled shyly.

Kenneth chuckled heartily. "This is very exciting, son! Very exciting! And I have all the confidence in the world that you and my daughter will do a wonderful job."

"Thank you, sir," Darryl said.

"We won't disappoint you, Father," Camryn interjected.

Kenneth moved to her side and wrapped his daughter in a deep bear hug. "Don't give this young man too hard a time," he said with a wink.

Camryn nodded, rolling her eyes. "So what is it we're supposed to be doing this afternoon, Mr. Boudreaux?" she asked.

He took a quick glance down at his wrist watch. "Actually, we have to be going," he said. "Gentlemen, it's been a pleasure. Camryn and I will keep you both updated."

Mason nodded his appreciation. "Kenneth, can I interest you in a late lunch?"

"Sounds like the best way to celebrate!" he answered.

As the two men led the way out of the room, Darryl hesitated, his gaze meeting Camryn's. The woman was eyeing him keenly. His mouth lifted easily, a margin of a smile warming his face.

"I've arranged for us to do a site tour. I think it will be of benefit to us both."

"I've been to the site already," Camryn responded curtly, her arms crossing over her chest.

Darryl sighed heavily, his gaze narrowing into thin slits.

Camryn tossed up her hands as if in surrender. "My apologies! I didn't mean that the way it sounded."

"Apology accepted. And I know you've already toured the site. So have I. But I thought that it would be useful for us to do an aerial tour. I was thinking about what you said yesterday about the aesthetic value of the design, and with the proposed height of the building, I thought that our looking at it from the air would be helpful."

"I hadn't thought about that," Camryn said.

"Finally!" Darryl exclaimed as he pretended to slap his forehead. "Something you hadn't considered!"

Camryn giggled softly and Darryl couldn't help but laugh with her.

The laughter didn't last long. The ride to Crescent City Helicopter was teeming with friction. Despite her best efforts, Camryn had initiated the first fight when Darryl had insisted on driving them in his car to their destination. Camryn had insisted on driving her own vehicle, a move Darryl had deemed a ridiculous waste of gasoline. Irate, Camryn had called him a fool, believing she knew better than he ever would. But after a heated back-and-forth Darryl had prevailed.

From start to finish Camryn had been unable to verbalize that riding in a car with him, alone, would cause more angst to her feminine spirit than she wanted to deal with. Darryl made her hot, point blank. And there was no amount of cool air or ice water capable of extinguishing the fire that burned from the pith of her crotch as he sat so closely by her side. So no, she hadn't wanted to ride in his car, nor did she want to be so close to him

in that darn helicopter, but there she was, seated so near
to him that the sweet scent of his cologne was beginning to make her dizzy with desire. She sighed as the
R44 Raven soared through the sky, dipping down low
against the New Orleans skyline. Turning her attention
to the views outside, she whispered a silent prayer that
they would soon be done and finished.

The gesture did not go unnoticed as Darryl took
a deep inhale. He cut an eye at her, distracted by the
exuberance across her face. She was so intoxicatingly
beautiful that it completely unnerved him. It unsettled
him because just minutes earlier she'd been so conten-
tious. She'd pouted and flailed over every suggestion
he had made. But he was even more frustrated by the
rise of desire that loomed heavier and heavier with each
minute they spent together.

He watched as her eyes skated across the landscape,
the woman clearly enamored with the experience. He'd
gotten it right and it was painted over every square inch
of her body. The joy she exuded had him grinning from
ear to ear.

The helicopter soared high along the cloudless skyline, navigating the airway over New Orleans. In the
distance the sun was just beginning to make its descent,
the edge of light reaching to kiss the mighty Mississippi, the brilliant rays dancing over the water's surface.

"It's absolutely beautiful!" Camryn gushed, her gaze
darting eagerly over the landscape.

Darryl turned to stare at her. *Yes, you are,* he thought
to himself, his own gaze dancing along her profile as
he noted her high cheekbones, dark, seductive eyes and

those full, lush lips. Her eyes flitted briefly toward him, hesitating for a quick moment before she looked away.

There was something seductive and intoxicating about the man's stare. Camryn struggled not to meet his gaze, knowing that nothing good could ever come from her staring into Darryl's eyes. Yet the look of longing he was giving her persisted.

"What do you know about my family, Darryl?" she suddenly asked, still looking out the helicopter window.

"Excuse me?"

"Our history. What do you know about it?"

Darryl shrugged his broad shoulders. "I know that you and your family come from a long line of architects."

She nodded ever so slightly. Closing her eyes, Camryn took a deep breath before continuing, drawing on the family stories that she'd been told since she was a little girl. "My mother was a Toutant before she married into the Charles family."

At the mention of the Toutant family name Darryl's eyebrows lifted curiously. The Toutant family was legendary, their lineage going back to the early 1700s when immigrants first took refuge in the newly established New Orleans. The infamous Lucian Toutant, son of a wealthy Parisian architect, had been an instrumental player in the development of the Vieux Carré, or French Quarter, as it was now known. Darryl leaned forward as she continued, not wanting to miss a word over the loud hum of the helicopter's engine.

"I'm sure you know that the French Quarter was composed of eight streets in a perfect square. And most of the architecture in the area was built during the time of Spanish rule. Some of the old French colonial influences were lost after the big fires of 1788 and 1794. Lucian Toutant's business ventures financed a significant portion of that rebuilding."

Turning to stare where Camryn pointed, Darryl could just imagine the views back then. Having scoured thousands of old maps and street plans, he knew that within the boundaries of the old square, construction had been happening wherever they turned, high-ceilinged homes rising grandly from the rich earth beneath them. The massive white columns and the black ironwork that adorned balconies during that bygone era still existed. Young trees that had lined the length of walkways with newly sprouted branches now loomed large and full, limbs stretched sky-high. In the distance, along the Mississippi waterway, a cruise ship was now docked where cargo ships had once landed and unloaded their goods.

"And it was rumored that his wife, Alexandra Fortier, influenced a number of those designs?" Darryl queried.

Camryn nodded. "My great-great-great-great-grandparents left quite a mark on this city." Her gaze moved back to the sights below.

As the pilot gestured in his direction, indicating that it was time to end their adventure, Darryl reflected on the moment. He understood that the landscape of New Orleans had changed under the dynamics of Hurricane Katrina, the Category 5 storm that had flooded the whole of the city in 2005. The French Quarter was one of the few areas to remain substantially dry, experiencing minor flooding and wind damage. Areas outside the Quarter had not been so lucky. And with everything their beloved city had endured, Darryl was desperate to ensure that nothing the Boudreaux family ever did would negatively impact the home they loved so dearly.

He turned to stare at Camryn and was taken aback by the tears that misted her eyes. Leaning even closer to her, he dropped a heavy palm against her knee, squeezing her flesh with a firm touch. Camryn lifted her eyes to his, a generous smile stretching easily across her face.

"The only thing my grandparents loved more than each other and their family was this city," she said softly, "so we can't get this wrong, Darryl. We can't get this wrong."

As Camryn dropped her hand atop his hand, entwining her fingers between his fingers, Darryl smiled back, understanding sweeping between them.

Chapter 5

It had been just over two weeks since Darryl had last seen Camryn. But before he'd departed, Darryl had dropped her back to her car after the helicopter ride. The two had spent another three hours just sitting in the front seat of his car talking before they parted ways. Conversation between them had been as easy as breathing.

Camryn had regaled him with stories of the Toutant clan and the historic plantation that now housed the Charles family. The sons and daughters of Toutant Plantation epitomized their auspicious beginnings. They were a family of "Creoles"—people of Spanish and French descent—and transient "Americans" who migrated from the North, as well as black slaves from Africa and the Caribbean, and members of the native Indian population. They were relationships that had crossed the ethnic divide, where family names and lineages might not have been preserved but true love always prevailed. Darryl had found himself enamored with the tales, which meshed historical fact with good old-fashioned homespun fiction.

Although he'd spoken to her every day, sometimes two and three times each day, he had not set eyes on her. Camryn had insisted on the distance, wanting to focus on her work without him or anyone else being a distraction, and so he'd given her a wide berth of space. But not one day had gone by that he did not talk with her, if for no other reason than to simply hear her voice.

Their conversations had sometimes crossed the boundaries of business, taking them to places that neither had expected to go. Darryl thoroughly enjoyed each encounter, whether they were laughing over something superficial or being rancorous over something substantial.

And when time had allowed, Darryl had found himself researching everything he could about Camryn Charles, reading articles from *Architectural Digest* and the society page of the *Times-Picayune*. Because despite his best efforts to resist, thoughts of Camryn Charles had invaded not only his waking moments but also his late-night dreams. Truth be told, he missed her terribly and the veracity of that burdened him even more.

With a picnic basket and thermos in hand, he rode the elevator to the third floor of the Tchoupitoulas Street address. The security guard waved him through. As Darryl entered the brick-and-glass office space, he instantly spotted Camryn pacing back and forth between two rooms. The minute he spied her Darryl broke out into a full and magnificent grin. He'd missed her even more than he'd realized. Glancing down to the Citizen watch on his wrist, he couldn't believe that Camryn was still in her office. When he'd called her shortly after seven that morning, she'd just gotten to her office. Now it was well past the dinner hour and she hadn't left. Darryl had no doubts that Camryn was past ready for a break. Taking a quick breath, he knocked before entering, announcing his arrival so as not to startle her.

But that knock caught her completely off guard. When she turned and saw him, Camryn's hands flew to her head first, her fingers patting down a few stray strands of loose hair, and then to her chest, clutching at the neckline of her ratty T-shirt. Her eyes rolled skyward, the expression across her face illustrating her displeasure. She'd been anxiously awaiting his evening telephone call, a conversation that she had come to look forward to each day, but seeing him was a horse of a whole other color. Darryl Boudreaux was the last man she had expected to see at such a late hour. She'd spoken to him early that afternoon and he had not mentioned anything about paying her a visit. If he had, she would have surely changed her clothes and done her makeup.

"Hey!" Darryl chimed, fighting not to laugh out loud at the expression that blessed her face.

Camryn's eyes were wide with surprise. "What are you doing here?"

He lifted the basket and thermos in greeting. "You need some nourishment," he said. "I told your assistant that I would surprise you with a home-cooked meal."

She eyed him with reservation. "You brought me dinner?"

"Lunch and breakfast, too, from what I'm told."

Camryn tossed a quick glance over her right shoulder, her hands gliding down the front of her denim jeans. "I really wasn't expecting company," she said, hesitancy still ringing in her tone.

Darryl shrugged. "Don't think of me as company. Think of me as family," he said as he moved past her, easing his way to the large conference table in the room.

After carefully assessing the surroundings, Darryl moved into a far corner. Camryn watched as he pulled a red-checked tablecloth from the basket and laid it neatly against the carpeted floor. As if setting a picnic meal was something he did every day, he laid out a spread of dinner plates, wineglasses, a collection of plastic containers and, lastly, one of the prettiest flameless LED candles that she had ever seen.

He looked over his shoulder, meeting her curious stare. "Are you going to come eat or are you going to just stand there twitching?" he said.

Camryn's eyes widened, one hand flying to pat her hair down again and the fingers of the other hand pressing against her face. "I wasn't twitching," she snarled.

Darryl laughed. "Yes, you were." He dropped down onto the floor, settling himself comfortably.

"I really need to get back to work," Camryn said impatiently.

"You need a break," Darryl persisted, gesturing for her to come take the seat beside him.

Feeling slightly defeated, Camryn inhaled swiftly and then crossed over to the other side of the room. She dropped down onto her knees at his side as she watched him pour white wine into a crystal flute and pass it to her.

"Thank you," Camryn said as Darryl poured a second drink for himself. That easy smile he wore so well crossed his face.

"You're very welcome," he responded, "and I hope you're hungry. I cooked and packed a lot of food."

She eyed him suspiciously. "You cooked?"

"You're about to find out that I'm quite talented in the kitchen, Ms. Charles. I've made you a down-home Cajun meal."

A wry grin pulled at Camryn's mouth as she popped the lid on one of the plastic containers. The decadent scent of shrimp gumbo filled her nostrils. Her grin widened when she opened the other container to find red beans and smoked sausage inside.

"Really? Red beans and no rice?"

Darryl laughed. "I done the rice, girl!" he said with a deep chuckle as he passed a third container toward her.

Suddenly famished, Camryn packed her plate full, eating heartily. Amused, Darryl watched her, slowly eating his own meal. After a few minutes of silence he laughed out loud. "I'm glad you weren't hungry!" he said teasingly.

Camryn's head waved from side to side. "It's good, okay? Give a girl a break!" She wiped her fingers and then her lips against a white paper napkin.

Darryl nodded, satisfaction painting his expression. He reached to refill her wineglass. "So how's it going? I hear you've been burning more than a little bit of midnight oil."

Excitement shimmered deep in Camryn's eyes. "It's been amazing," she answered. "Once I started drawing, I couldn't stop. After our helicopter ride, when I began to do some preliminary sketches, it just hit me. I think you and your brother will be very happy."

"So do you have something I can see?" Darryl asked.

Camryn paused as if the question startled her. "Well...I... It's..." she stammered.

Darryl shook his head. "No interference. I promise. I'm just excited to see in what direction you decided to take your design."

He smiled that disarming smile and Camryn could feel herself starting to melt. After pondering his request for a quick second she figured one little peek at her blueprints couldn't hurt.

"Well, I guess you could," she said softly, hardly sounding convinced.

Darryl grinned. "Would a bribe help you decide?" he questioned, his eyebrows raised.

"What kind of bribe?"

Darryl reached into the picnic basket and pulled out one more plastic container. He cracked open the lid and peered inside. The way he peeked with one eye closed and then peered up at her, one would have thought it held a great secret.

Camryn reached for the container and Darryl snatched it back from her grasp. With his eyebrows lifted and his smile widening, his mischievous expression made her laugh.

"You want this?" he teased.

"I want to know what's in it," she said. "I may not like what's inside."

"Oh, you'll like it!"

Camryn reached for the container a second time. There was a playful tug-of-war before Darryl let go and

Camryn fell back from the momentum. When Darryl laughed, Camryn shot him a look that clearly showed she was not amused by his antics.

He reached out to help her sit back up. "Sorry about that."

"You pushed me!"

"I did not!"

"Yes, you did!"

Darryl laughed. "Okay."

"That's my story and I'm sticking to it," Camryn said as she cut her eyes at him. She settled the container against her lap and lifted the lid. Her own smile widened. "Pecan pralines!"

"Homemade pecan pralines."

"You did not make these," Camryn said as she bit into what would be the first of many.

"I beg your pardon!"

"Your mother cooked all this food and you're taking credit for it, right?"

"Wrong!" His expression was incredulous. "Very wrong!"

Camryn smiled brightly and Darryl smiled with her. The two sat staring at each other for a brief moment before Camryn lifted herself onto her feet and gestured for him to follow. She was still holding tight to the candy container, savoring the sweetness of the sugared delights.

Leading the way back to her office, Camryn motioned for Darryl to flip through the sketches and blueprints laid out across the table. As he stepped forward, his expression turning serious, she was suddenly excited for him to see what she'd accomplished.

"I wanted it to be reflective of the city's history. And I didn't want it to be just another modernist skyscraper like those in the Central Business District. But with the proposed height, I had to figure out how to marry a contemporary style and a traditional style and make them work together. It was a challenge but I'm really pleased with the results."

Darryl tossed her a quick glance before leaning over the table to take a closer look at one of the blueprints. His silence was unnerving and Camryn bit down against her bottom lip as she anticipated his critique.

"It reminds me of the grand mansions on St. Charles Avenue. It's very Queen Anne–like but then because of its size, it's not."

"I'm impressed. You got it."

"Not as much as I am. Are you drawing the structural blueprints, as well? Did you really detail the steel framing by hand, not CAD software?"

"I'm very good at what I do, Mr. Boudreaux," she said, passing him one of the pralines. "Of course, I expect you to make sure they're correct. The load bearings need to be detailed precisely and I hear that's your specialty."

Darryl took a bite of the sweet confection as he nodded his head. He lifted the blueprint, staring at the details more closely. "This is good work, Camryn. Really good," he said, turning to meet her gaze.

Camryn felt herself break out into a sudden sweat. Darryl's close proximity was definitely more than she could bear. She thought about her hair being all over her head and her face lacking even a hint of foundation or lipstick. She had to be one hot mess standing there in torn jeans and a ragged T-shirt.

Before she could catch it, the container in her hand fell to the floor, the last piece of candy rolling under the office desk. Her eyes widened as she dropped down onto her hands and knees, grappling to retrieve the treat.

"Damn," Camryn cursed, muttering cuss words under her breath.

Dropping down beside her, Darryl laughed. "Need some help?"

"No...I can..." she stammered, words catching in her throat. She shook her head and dropped down onto her backside, her legs extended out in front of her. She crossed her ankles. "That piece of candy was yours," she said finally, lifting her gaze to his.

Darryl laughed. "No, my candy is *safely* in a plastic container in the basket," he said, sitting down beside her. He dropped a casual arm over her shoulder as he continued to laugh heartily.

Before Camryn knew it, she was laughing with him, the booming chuckle rising from deep in her midsection. Tears pressed at the backs of her eyelids, the contagious moment spreading from one to the other. Like a refreshing thunderstorm, the laughter washed away the last bit of anxiety she'd been feeling.

Eventually their breathing slowed and the two settled comfortably in the moment. Camryn couldn't remember the last time she'd laughed so hard or been so relaxed. Despite her initial reservations she was glad that Darryl had come by bearing food. The break had been a nice reprieve and seeing him was like icing on top of the tastiest cake. Everything suddenly felt in sync just because he was there in the flesh, by her side. She rested her head against his shoulder.

"Thank you," Camryn said. "I guess I needed this."

"You're very welcome. I needed it, as well," Darryl replied. His large hand gently massaged her shoulder.

Camryn hated to admit that she actually felt quite comfortable in his arms. Too comfortable. She turned her head to stare up at him, her gaze following the lines of his profile. The precision cut of his beard and mustache was sexy as hell. Much too sexy. Camryn fought to stall the heat that billowed between them. Just as Darryl stared down at her, she shifted her body from his, lifting herself out of his arms. "I really need to get back to work," she said, that anxiety returning swiftly.

"Really?" Darryl asked. He watched as she scurried to her feet.

"Yes. And you need to leave."

"Why?"

Camryn shifted nervously but before she could respond, the harsh jingle of Darryl's cell phone rang from his pocket.

"Hold that thought," he said, holding up an index finger in pause. His gaze shifted from her face down to the appliance as he pulled it into his hands. The expression across his face suddenly swung from relaxed to tense as his gaze shot back to her and then to his phone. He silenced the ringer, attempting to ignore the call. An uncomfortable silence seemed to suddenly consume the room.

"Is something wrong?" Camryn inquired, eyeing him suspiciously.

Darryl shook his head. His phone rang a second time. "I apologize," he said. "I need to take this."

Camryn watched as he sprinted from the room, clutching the cell phone to his ear. "Hello?"

Out in the hallway his voice was muffled and Camryn was only able to decipher a word or two of the conversation. But those few words were enough to pique her curiosity. Minutes later when Darryl returned, she had shifted into investigator mode. "Is everything okay?"

"Fine." His nervousness was evident as he struggled not to meet her gaze. "I guess I should be going," Darryl said abruptly.

Camryn nodded her head. "Girlfriend checking up on you, huh?"

"Excuse me?"

She pointed at the cell phone he was twisting nervously beneath his palm. "That call. It sounded like your girlfriend was checking up on you. Asia?"

He shook his head. "Asia is not my girlfriend. I don't have one."

"Really?"

He smiled ever so slightly. "Really. It was just an old friend in need of some assistance. And why were you eavesdropping on my telephone call?"

"So it was a booty call!" Camryn exclaimed, ignoring his question.

He rolled his eyes as he shook his head. "It was not a booty call, Camryn."

"Then why are you blushing?"

"I don't blush," Darryl said, knowing his cheeks were heated with color.

"Hey, it's okay," she said, trying to sound indifferent.

"I mean, you're single, so if a female friend was looking for some attention, there would be nothing wrong with that." She shrugged her shoulders nonchalantly.

Darryl took a step in her direction. He smiled smugly. "I like a woman who can joke around, Ms. Charles. And you've got jokes."

Camryn took a step back. "No jokes here," she said, a wry smile crossing her face. "I was being very serious!"

Darryl took a second step forward. The grin on his face was like lighter fluid, igniting a rage of heat between them. It was so intense that Camryn thought she might actually combust. She pressed her knees together, closing the space between her thighs. She instinctively wanted to back up to put as much distance between them as she could muster but she didn't. Standing like stone, she stood her ground as she met his intense stare and held it.

Darryl nodded and chuckled softly. "I had fun tonight, Ms. Charles."

"Me, too," she said with a slight nod of her own.

"You and I make a great team," Darryl stated.

Camryn shrugged her shoulders.

Darryl was about to take another step forward when his phone rang a third time. He quickly silenced the device and apologized. "Sorry."

"Don't be," Camryn answered. "Duty calls."

Darryl eyed her with amusement, the all-knowing expression on her face moving him to grin even wider. "Do you have plans tomorrow?" he asked.

Camryn nodded her head. "More work, sir."

"Sounds like a plan," Darryl responded. "I'll bring dinner." Then he turned and disappeared down the hall.

Chapter 6

Asia. Camryn couldn't help but wonder who Asia was and if Darryl might actually be headed to see this women he called a friend. Asia had been anxious for his attention. Camryn couldn't help but reason that a friend might have called once but a significant other might have been more insistent. Whoever this Asia was…she was definitely more than a simple late-night booty call, Camryn rationalized.

She sighed heavily. It wasn't as if she should care, but she did. The thought was actually disturbing because she shouldn't care an ounce about Darryl Boudreaux's private life. And she shouldn't have been wasting her time wondering whether or not he was headed to another woman's bed.

Despite the hours of conversation they'd shared, not once had she asked him about his personal life. It would have been unprofessional, Camryn thought. And if she was honest with herself, she hadn't really wanted to know. She would have been crushed if Darryl had admitted to having someone special in his life. Someone else he made picnic lunches for and called all hours of the day and night to talk to. Camryn enjoyed thinking she was the only woman who had the man's attention, even if it was only for business.

She snatched the plastic container from the corner of the table where she had rested it and moved back to where Darryl had set up their dinner. Gathering the plates and cutlery, she tossed everything back inside the basket, not caring how neat or organized it was. She spied that last plastic container almost by accident.

Dropping back down to the floor, Camryn pulled the container into her lap, snapping the lid open easily. She couldn't help but wonder what a taste of Darryl Boudreaux's treats might do for her, and the scandalous thoughts were as delicious as his candy.

Darryl had been having a good time. Actually, he'd been having a *great* time with Camryn. Asia calling him out of the blue had been unexpected and unwanted, the woman insisting they needed to talk. Like everything with Asia, what she wanted and needed took precedence over everything and everyone else.

He still didn't have a clue about what they needed to talk about. In his mind everything that needed to be said had been spoken the night she shot holes in his wall. He didn't have anything else to say. But when his phone rang again, he knew that Asia apparently had a lot that she wanted to get off her chest.

"Hello?"

"Please don't hang up on me, Darryl," Asia Landry intoned. "Please."

"What do you want, Asia?"

"I just want to apologize. I need you to understand that I wasn't in my right mind when I pulled that gun."

"That's fine, Asia."

"Is it really? Do you really forgive me?"

Darryl took a deep breath and held it.

Asia continued. "I go to court tomorrow. My attorney has asked for a plea deal."

Darryl exhaled sharply. "Asia, why are you calling me? I mean, really. What is there for us to say to each other?"

"I love you, Darryl. I would never have done anything to hurt you. I need you to know that."

There was a moment of pause as Asia waited for him to respond. When he didn't say anything, she persisted. "We were so good together, Darryl. I miss that. I'm so sorry that I let my jealousy ruin our relationship. I can do better. I'm going to counseling and I want us to work out. I really do. I still love you!"

"I don't see that happening, Asia. I appreciate your apology and I wish you all the best but being in a relationship with each other is just not a good thing for either of us. Individually, you and I are spectacular. Together, we are toxic to the extreme. It's not healthy for me and it's not healthy for you, either."

The woman bristled on the other end, the sting of his words like a harsh slap. "I understand," she said finally. "But I think we just need some time apart. I have high hopes for us, Darryl. I really do."

Darryl nodded into the receiver. "Please don't call me anymore, Asia. Please."

"Anything you want, Darryl," she responded. "I love you!"

"Goodbye, Asia," he said as he hung up.

Darryl sighed deeply as he maneuvered his car through downtown New Orleans. He hoped that goodbye would be the last and that he and Asia were done for good. Despite her persistence, Asia Landry was not the woman he was thinking about. Because not thinking about Camryn Charles was proving to be nearly impossible.

The beautiful woman consumed his thoughts and seeing her had only served to further fuel his interest. As long as he had anything to say about it, never again would so much time lapse without them seeing each other. If he had his way, he was going to make sure that he saw Camryn every day.

Camryn Charles was quickly becoming a very sweet addiction.

Chapter 7

Maitlyn Parks was almost shouting into her cell phone receiver. Standing outside the Los Angeles courthouse, she battled the noise of traffic and pedestrians around her, everyone fighting to be heard.

"A slap on the wrist! They gave that girl a slap on the wrist for trying to kill you!"

On the other end, Darryl shook his head from side to side. "It was her first offense. The district attorney told me they were going to give her a plea deal and that she'd probably just get probation."

"And that's all she got. Her father's money bailed her out again."

"Well, it's done and finished, Mattie. Let it go."

"I will not. The girl tried to *kill* you. She should be doing some hard time."

"She called me last night to apologize."

"She what?" Maitlyn screamed. "That's a violation of your restraining order. Why didn't you report it?"

"Because I want this over with, Maitlyn. I need to focus on my work and this project, not Asia Landry. Reporting it would have just made the situation worse. I don't need this mess to be any worse."

Maitlyn audibly sighed. "Her father came over to apologize. He said to tell you that Asia won't be a problem anymore."

"Mr. Landry has always been optimistic when it comes to Asia."

"Mr. Landry has always been a fool when it comes to Asia. I don't know about optimistic."

"I've got to get back to work, Maitlyn. Thank you for handling that for me."

"You're welcome," his sister answered. "And you know I'm going away for a while, right?"

"Yeah, I heard. Something about a cruise, right?"

"A thirty-four-day transatlantic excursion to Spain and back. I can't wait."

"Wow! Thirty-four days! What will we ever do without you for that long?"

Maitlyn shrugged. "You'll survive. We Boudreauxs always do."

"Enjoy your trip," Darryl said. "And have one of those fruity drinks with an umbrella in it for me."

Maitlyn laughed. "For you, little brother, I'll have two!"

As Darryl disconnected the call and stepped back into the conference room, he felt Camryn staring at him. He lifted his gaze to meet hers.

"What?"

"Nothing," Camryn responded, pulling her eyes from his.

"No, it's something," he said teasingly. "If you've got something to say, woman, just spit it out."

Camryn held up a hand. "It's none of my business," she said. Inside, she had so many questions that curiosity was choking the life out of the cat.

Darryl dropped down onto a cushioned office chair. "No, it's not your business but you still want to know. Look at you! Just like last night, you're anxious to know what I was talking about and who I was talking to!"

She rolled her eyes. "Oh, please! I wasn't even paying attention to your conversation or your booty call last night."

Darryl smiled. "Okay."

She looked at him, not at all amused by his teasing. "Whatever."

Darryl chuckled softly. He leaned forward in his seat, his forearms resting on his thighs, his hands clasped tightly together. His expression turned serious. "My ex-girlfriend, Asia Landry, was put on probation today for discharging a firearm inside my home. My sister was there for the hearing and just wanted to fill me in."

"Asia Landry?" Recognition furrowed Camryn's brow. "Not Asia Landry of the James Landry Group?"

Darryl nodded. "James Landry's daughter. Do you know her?"

"I know her work. And his. James Landry has an exceptional reputation in the industry. You worked for him for a while, didn't you?" Camryn questioned, fragments of Darryl's résumé coming back to her.

He nodded. "I did. Years before I dated his daughter."

"How long were you two together?"

"Not long at all really. There was a lot of back-and-forth in the relationship. I officially broke things off a few times over the last year but we still had a few issues between us."

"Sounds like it if the woman was shooting at you."

Darryl shook his head. "She wasn't shooting at me!"

"Lucky for you she missed."

He laughed again. "Okay, so that's all of my dirty secrets. What about yours?"

"I don't have any secrets. And I definitely don't have a jealous boyfriend trying to shoot me."

"Well, that's good," Darryl countered.

"Why is that good?"

Darryl grinned. "It just is," he said smugly. He leaned forward and grabbed her hand beneath his, caressing her fingers softly.

Camryn laughed. "Oh, no, you don't," she said, pulling her hand from his. "We're just becoming friends, Darryl Boudreaux. It's not going any further than that and I mean it."

"I don't know what you're talking about," Darryl said coyly. "I make it my policy not to mix business with pleasure, Ms. Charles." He met her gaze. His teasing stare felt like a soft caress.

The silence was awkward, Camryn feeling just a hair shy of foolish for even implying that Darryl might have wanted anything more. And then he reached for her hand again, his touch telling her something different.

Camryn bit down on her bottom lip, snatching her hand away a second time. "I mean it, Darryl!"

"Okay," he said, his tone still smug. Then he winked an eye at her, causing a ruffle of heat to waft up her spine.

Camryn had no idea what had possessed her to call him. But she had, waiting until just before noon to dial Darryl's number and casually ask about budget numbers. The question had been random and she could hear in his tone that he knew she had no interest in his budget. Then she asked him what it was she really wanted from him.

"Do you play racquetball?" Camryn asked.

"I've been on the court before. Why?"

"I need to get some exercise."

Darryl chuckled. "I think I can help you out with that! Where do you play?"

"The Elmwood Fitness Center down in Harahan."

"Can I rent a racquet?"

"I have an extra you can borrow."

"I can be ready in an hour," Darryl said. "But you have to drive."

She laughed. "I don't mind driving. I'll see you in about an hour."

Forty minutes later Camryn was sitting in her car, the air conditioning running on high while she anticipated Darryl sitting in the seat beside her. The man still made her stomach quiver with butterflies when they were in close proximity of each other. The fluttering had started when she'd dialed his number. It had revved up the second he'd agreed to play racquetball with her. And sitting in the Roosevelt Hotel's parking lot anticipating them being in each other's company had her stomach on overload. She was desperately hoping to use the time to get a grip on her nerves. Glancing at the clock on the dashboard, she figured she'd give herself a good ten-minute pep talk before calling him down to meet her.

She was fantasizing about the two of them, imagining them naked together, when there was a sudden knock on the passenger-side window. Camryn jumped, completely startled from her thoughts. She looked over to see Darryl peering into the window. He pulled open the car door and slid inside, tossing his sports bag to the backseat.

"You could have called. If I hadn't come down to get my sneakers out of my car, I would still be upstairs thinking you weren't here."

Camryn shook her head. "I was trying to give you a full hour. I would have called when I was ready for you."

"Oh! You want me to get out?" Darryl dropped his hand to the door handle.

"You're here now," she quipped, laughter dancing in her eyes.

"We need to talk about your attitude," Darryl teased.

"My attitude? I don't have an attitude!"

He gestured toward the car keys. "I beg to differ but we'll discuss it on the ride. Let's get rolling."

"And you're giving orders!" Camryn exclaimed as she shifted the car into Drive and pulled out into traffic.

Darryl laughed heartily. "I'm glad you called. I needed to get away."

"Is business wearing you down?"

"It has just taken a lot to put everything in order.

Once we break ground, the schedule will ease up substantially. Then it'll just be ensuring the builder is on schedule and double-checking behind the inspectors."

"You have a wonderful design, so I'm sure it will all go smoothly," she responded. "You had a damn good architect, you know!"

He shook his head. "I'm sure."

The two laughed.

"So, how long have you been playing racquetball?" Darryl asked.

"For a few years now. And I'm very good, so you better be prepared to get your butt whopped. I plan to beat you down."

"You might take a beating," he chimed sarcastically. "I will not be beaten by a *woman.*"

"How chauvinistic of you!"

"Not at all. I don't have any problems with a woman flexing her moxie to prove she is just as good, or even better, than her male counterpart. However, *I* will just not be outdone by a woman."

"So, what you're saying is that a woman can't beat a man?" Camryn looked at Darryl inquisitively.

"I'm saying that a woman, specifically *you,* can't beat me. I can't, however, speak for my brethren and their women."

"Aren't you full of yourself?"

Darryl leaned back, his hands crossed behind his head. "Truth hurts."

"I've got truth for you!" Camryn laughed again.

The thirty-minute ride to Harahan was comfortable and easy. Darryl made her laugh and the butterflies in the pit of her stomach were floating comfortably. By the time they reached the gym, she was starting to question whether or not she could be focused enough to give Darryl a solid run for his smug money.

Camryn had reserved one of the three glass-enclosed racquetball courts for them at one of the premier racquetball-and-indoor-sports complexes in the Louisiana area. Darryl knew the minute she exited the women's locker room that he was in trouble. The black performance shorts she wore were too short and the matching tank top more than flattering to her full bustline and thin waist. He struggled not to stare, his jaw dropping to the floor when she stepped onto the court. He noticed that he wasn't the only appreciative eye in the gym.

The woman had an athletic frame of tightly toned muscles. More leg than torso, she had long limbs that seemed miles high. Her buttocks were round and full like oversize melons. Heat shifted in his groin as he suddenly imagined those legs spread in a wide V with him nestled waist-deep in the warm crevice. He suddenly realized he'd been holding his breath.

Camryn called his name, pulling him from the reverie.

"I'm sorry, what were you saying?"

She was staring at him with one hand on her hip. "I asked if you were ready to see who gets the first serve."

"Oh…yeah…I…yeah," he stammered, shaking the clouds from his head. "You go."

Camryn tossed him a wry smile. Taking aim, she rebounded the ball off the front wall, landing it near center of the dotted line on the floor. She turned and grinned, throwing him a ball from her pocket. "Your turn!"

Darryl took a deep breath and grinned back. He took his position and slammed the ball against the wall. It landed far from its target. He glanced at Camryn. "I think you get to serve first."

"I think you're right," she said as she pushed him out of her way.

Darryl laughed and tapped her on her backside, enjoying the easy jiggle of her buttocks.

Camryn faulted on her first serve.

It was a back-and-forth match that had them both sweating profusely for over an hour. On the last set, Darryl played hard and Camryn played harder. Darryl missed her last slam by mere inches. Throwing her arms in the air, she cheered excitedly, jumping up and down. Her exuberance was contagious and Darryl couldn't help but smile. He bowed slowly, gesturing with one hand sweeping outward, the other held behind his back.

"Congratulations!"

"Fifteen!" Camryn cheered. "I won! I beat you!"

Darryl shrugged. "Best two out of three?"

"Awww! Does the big man need to play more than two games to beat the little lady?"

Darryl laughed. "Can I at least buy you dinner, then?"

"And dessert. You're buying dessert, too," she said matter-of-factly.

Darryl nodded his agreement. "Dessert, too, then."

"I'm going to grab a quick shower. I'll meet you in the lobby," she said.

He watched as Camryn headed toward the locker room, her full hips switching nicely in those shorts. She reached the room door and paused, giving him a look over her shoulder. Her stare took his breath away. He called out to her.

"Yes?"

"You do know that I *let* you win! It won't happen again."

She tossed him a nod of her head. "Darryl Boudreaux! You didn't *let* me do anything!"

She razzed him through their first cocktail, the appetizers and halfway through the entrée. Her kidding was all in good fun and Darryl took it admirably.

"You're thoroughly enjoying this, aren't you?" Darryl said with a hearty chuckle.

"Yes, I am," Camryn said, laughing. "In fact, I can't wait to tell everyone. I figure I'll start with the boys down at the construction site. Then, of course, it's going to make great conversation around the water cooler at Charles & Charles." She smirked.

"Don't stop there. I'm thinking you should just put up a webpage with a link for everyone to just replay that last shot over and over again."

"Webpage, billboards, full-page ads… I'm thinking the sky's the limit!" Camryn exclaimed.

Darryl rolled his eyes playfully. He rested his gaze on her face. Her hair was still damp from her shower, the lush strands pulled back into a tight ponytail. A few tendrils curled around her face. She took his breath away.

"You beat me fair and square. It was a good challenge."

"I caught a cramp when we tied that first time. You almost had me then."

"Yes, I did!"

"Almost."

"Did you know that you are quite beautiful when you're being pompous?"

Camryn smiled. "Pompous?"

Darryl leaned forward ever so slightly. The gesture gave Camryn reason to pause as she instinctively shifted toward him. His face was mere inches from hers, his lips close to her lips as he stared into her eyes. His smile was sweet and welcoming. He brushed a hand down her cheek, his fingers lightly gracing her profile as he pushed a curl out of her eye. When he suddenly leaned back and away from her, she had to struggle to keep the disappointment out of her eyes.

Chapter 8

"Why doesn't the contractor have final copies of the blueprints?" Camryn asked, the question directed at her assistant.

"His copies were delivered weeks ago," the young woman answered.

"We break ground tomorrow and the man claims he doesn't have copies of the blueprints!"

"I delivered them personally, Ms. Charles. I assure you he has his copies." The assistant was wide-eyed and flustered.

Camryn tossed up her hands in frustration. "And who picked this crew?" she asked, shooting a look toward Darryl.

He grinned sheepishly, throwing up his own hands. "What can I say? Good help is sometimes hard to find," Darryl said jokingly in an attempt to make her laugh.

They were becoming fast friends. And with each

passing day, the bond between them was growing stronger. Darryl was delighted to be able to work so closely with Camryn. The intelligent woman was mesmerizing, her talents beyond his wildest imagination. She challenged and inspired his own work. Side by side the two of them were giving life to his brother's vision, the magnanimous building taking on a life of its own, much as the friendship between them was becoming corporeal.

And she had the most intoxicating laugh of any woman he had ever known. He loved to hear her laugh, the wealth of it always seeming to start somewhere deep in her midsection. When she laughed, there was nothing else he could do but laugh with her.

In that moment, though, Camryn wasn't doing much laughing. Since Darryl had arrived at the office, she'd been bellowing one order after another.

"I really can't believe—"

Darryl interrupted her. "Calm down, Camryn. The contractor is one of the best in the business. You've also called him a half dozen times since I got here this morning, which means you've annoyed him more than a dozen times today and it's barely 9:00 a.m."

"Am I the only one trying to do my job?" Camryn snapped. "The man insists he never received the blueprints!"

"Knowing Gerald, I'm sure he told you he didn't have the blueprints to give you something else to focus on so that you would leave him alone. Obviously he has the blueprints, because he acquired all the building permits. You can't get permits without blueprints."

"Am I the only one concerned about us breaking ground tomorrow?"

Darryl directed a look at Camryn's assistant and shrugged his shoulders. His grin was miles wide and the woman smiled with him. He gestured with his head and she excused herself from the room, leaving Darryl and Camryn alone together.

"As project manager on this project, I can personally assure you that we will break ground with no problems, Ms. Charles."

"You really need to take this seriously," Camryn stated, her hands resting on her hips.

Darryl chuckled. "I am very serious when I say that you are officially overworked and in need of a break."

"I don't have time—"

"Make time," Darryl commanded. He looked down at his watch. "We leave in ten minutes."

"To where? I'm not going—"

"Ten minutes," Darryl interrupted.

Camryn bristled. As she sat fuming, her assistant poked her head into the room.

"Ms. Charles, the contractor said he found the blueprints and everything is right on schedule."

Camryn hadn't muttered ten words to him the entire ride. And not because she didn't have anything to say but because she needed every ounce of her energy to stall the rise of wanting that threatened to consume her.

With the bright sunshine raining down and the warm temperatures rising steadily, Darryl had lowered the top on his late-model convertible rental, the breeze ruffling Camryn's lush curls. He eased the vehicle uptown into the Fourteenth Ward. Although he'd anticipated a host of questions from her, she'd not asked him again where they were going. It was only when he pulled past the wrought-iron gates of the Boudreaux Broadway Street home that she cut her eye at him, a wave of anxiety filling the pit of her stomach. Her eyes widened.

"Where are we?" she questioned, eyeing him with reservation.

Darryl smiled. "My home."

"But you're staying with your parents, right? Is this their home?"

Darryl nodded. "Yes, it is. I need to pick something up."

"Are your parents home?"

"Probably," Darryl said as he shifted the car into Park and shut down the engine. "Is that a problem?"

"You could have warned me that I'd be meeting your parents," she said. She pulled down the sun visor to check her makeup in the mirror.

Darryl laughed. "Why? We're just friends, right? It shouldn't be a big deal."

The look Camryn gave him was hostile at best. She adjusted her clothes and pulled her hands through her hair.

"There you go fidgeting," Darryl said, eyeing her back.

"I'm not fidgeting," Camryn said beneath clenched teeth.

Exiting the vehicle, Darryl moved to the passenger side of the car and opened the door. He extended a hand in her direction. Camryn stared up at him, still put out by the fact that she was meeting his parents without notice. She glared and Darryl tossed her a look back.

"What, Camryn?"

"Nothing!" she snapped.

"So, are you coming?" he asked, extending his hand a second time.

Pushing his hand away, Camryn made her own way out of the car, slamming the door behind her. She motioned for him to lead the way.

Darryl laughed as he turned an about-face and headed for the front door. His parents met them at the entrance.

"Hello, Son-shine!"

"Good morning, Mom," Darryl said as he kissed his mother's cheek before extending his hand toward his father. "Welcome back, sir! How was your trip?"

Mason "Senior" Boudreaux shook his son's hand, then pulled him into a hearty embrace. "The trip was good. We had a great time with those grandbabies."

"Well, it's good to have you back."

"Thank you for keeping the house clean," his mother said. "I was sure I was going to come back to a mess."

Darryl's father looked past his son's shoulder, spying Camryn, who was standing nervously on the top step. "Darryl, where are your manners? Folks would think you have had no home training. Good morning, pretty lady!" Mason Senior chimed, holding out his hand. "Mason Boudreaux, but everyone calls me Senior," he said as he pumped Camryn's arm up and down. "Introduce your friend, boy!"

Darryl threw a glance over his shoulder. "Oh, that's

Camryn. Camryn Charles, these are my parents…my mother, Katherine, and my father, Senior."

Katherine wrapped Camryn in a warm hug. "So, you're Camryn. It's very nice to meet you, dear. Darryl talks about you all the time!"

"Thank you," Camryn said, a smile brightening her face. "It's nice to meet you both, as well."

"I don't talk about her all the time," Darryl muttered under his breath.

Katherine laughed. "Oh, yes, you do," she said, still holding on to Camryn. "My son is a big fan of yours!" She gestured for the two of them to follow her into the house.

"We're not staying," Darryl said. "I just needed to pick up some paperwork and Camryn needed a break from the office."

"I hear my boys have you working hard on this building Mason is putting up," Senior interjected.

"Yes, sir. It's been very exciting and Mason has been a sheer joy to work with."

"I thought you've been working with Darryl?" Senior queried, looking from one to the other.

"I have," Camryn answered, a rush of color rising to her cheeks. "He's been something to work with, too!"

Darryl's parents eyed them both and then burst out laughing.

"Sounds to me like the honeymoon is officially over," Senior joked, hanging an arm over his wife's shoulder.

"Or just getting started," Katherine teased.

Darryl rolled his eyes. "Thank you, Mom and Dad. I am now officially embarrassed."

"Nothing to be embarrassed about, boy!" Senior exclaimed, tossing Camryn a wink of his eye. "Man can't help who he might be sweet on!"

Camryn giggled nervously. Darryl shot her a look before turning back to his parents.

"Camryn and I are just working together. She is only a friend," Darryl called over his shoulder as he headed up a flight of stairs. "Ask her! She set the rules!"

Camryn's face was flushed with embarrassment. "We... I... It's..." she stammered, not having a clue if she needed to respond.

Katherine laughed. "Don't pay my son or my husband an ounce of attention. You'll get used to it. Are you two hungry, dear? I can fix you something to eat."

"No, ma'am, but thank you for offering."

"Well, at least sit and have a cup of tea with me," Katherine said, motioning for Camryn to follow her into the kitchen.

Minutes later when Darryl bounded down the stairs, the two women had disappeared and Senior was sitting in his favorite recliner, flipping through the morning newspaper. "Where's Camryn?" he asked as he moved into the room.

Senior gestured with his head. "She's having a chat with your mother. She seems like a nice young lady. I know Mason speaks very highly of her."

Darryl smiled shyly. "She's okay."

"She doesn't seem as high-strung as that other girl you used to date. You know which one I'm talking about. That crazy one that tried to shoot you. The one the judge put on probation. You remember her, don't you?"

Darryl dropped his head back against his shoulders.

He took a deep breath and blew it out slowly. "Senior, I—" he started.

Mason Senior shook his head. "You need to handle your business, Darryl. You haven't cleaned up that situation yet and here you are all hot over another woman. Don't think we don't see the way you look at that girl."

"I like Camryn. I like Camryn a lot and things with Asia are over, so—"

His father cut him off a second time. "You want things with Asia to be over but trust me when I tell you over might not be that easy when a woman resorts to shooting at you."

"Senior, she didn't—"

Senior stalled his words again, holding up his hand. "I just need you to remember to be careful, son. Know a woman before you rush into anything. That's the problem with you young people today. Always want to rush into something and don't have a clue what you're dealing with. I had to tell your nephew Collin that just the other day. Much like you, that boy's nose is wide open over some young girl. Done had him a little tail and now you can't tell him anything. But these days you just can't be too careful."

"Little Collin?" Darryl questioned, thinking of his older sister Katrina's young son. "You're joking right?"

"Collin's not so little anymore. Boy's driving, about to graduate, and them hormones of his are raging. I told him about being so fast because these days some of the girls are faster than the boys. He's giving Matthew and Katrina a run for their money!"

Darryl laughed.

For the first time since their conversation started,

Mason Senior peered over the top of his newspaper to stare up at Darryl.

"It's not funny. That boy is about as bad as you were the first time you got you some! Don't think I don't remember that. What was that little girl's name? Pattie, Penny, Paula? Pauline! That was her. Pauline Satterwhite. She lived next door to your aunt Helen. You know I don't forget much!"

Darryl tossed a quick look over his shoulder. "Senior! Come on, man!"

"Just be smart, Darryl. That's all I'm saying."

Blowing out a gust of air, Darryl nodded his head. "Yes, sir!"

The two women moved back into the room, interrupting the conversation.

"What about Pauline Satterwhite?" Katherine asked. She directed her next comment at Camryn. "That was Darryl's first little girlfriend. She was a sweet girl but she was hot in the pants. I remember having to talk to her mama one day about her being so hot."

Camryn looked at him with raised eyebrows as his mother continued. "Darryl, when's the last time you saw that girl?"

He shook his head. "It's been years, mama. Senior was just trying to remember her name."

"What made you think about that girl, Senior?" she asked.

Her husband shrugged, not bothering to respond as he and Darryl locked eyes, the motion almost conspiratorial. Not missing the gesture, Katherine changed the subject.

"Darryl, do you want a cup of tea, Son-shine?"

"No, thanks, Mom. Camryn and I really have to be going," he said as Camryn moved back to his side.

"Well, definitely come back for dinner sometime soon," Katherine said. "You bring her back, Darryl," his mother admonished.

Darryl met Camryn's gaze. "Maybe, but she's going to have to start acting right first," he said.

Camryn's eyes widened. "I don't believe you," she gushed.

"I mean it," Darryl said. "You're too moody and when you get in one of your moods you're like a girl-zilla!"

"I am not!"

"Your mother gets that way, too," Senior said matter-of-factly. He twirled his index finger in the air.

Katherine looped her arm through Camryn's. "Don't pay either one of them an ounce of attention." She gave her husband a look. "You know you like it when I'm in one of my moods."

"Yes, I do, baby," Senior chuckled. "Yes, I do."

Then Katherine whispered into Camryn's ear. "Be moody if you want, honey. Keep 'em guessing. They like it when they don't know what's coming their way."

Camryn giggled. "Yes, ma'am."

"Be nice to this girl, Darryl. I like her," Katherine chided as she escorted them to the front door. "You hear me?"

"Yes, ma'am!" Darryl said as Camryn stuck her tongue out at him. His mouth flew open as he pointed a finger in her direction but no one seemed to catch her gesture.

Extending her goodbyes, Camryn headed back to

the car as Darryl hugged both of his parents. The couple waved from the porch. Darryl eased his way to her side, reaching to unlock the passenger-side door. He then opened it to let Camryn inside.

"I can't believe you did that to me," she said, spinning around to face him.

"Did what?"

She shook her head. "I can just imagine what your parents are thinking about me."

"They liked you."

"They were being nice."

"Yes, they were. Because they liked you. So what are you complaining about?"

He took a step toward her, standing so close that the sweet scent of his cologne teased her nostrils. Nerves suddenly had her quivering in her high heels. "I wasn't complaining," she murmured, fighting not to meet his gaze.

"Sounded like a complaint to me," Darryl said softly.

"Well, you're—" Camryn started.

Before she could finish, Darryl slipped a large hand around her waist, snaking it to the small of her back. Camryn's eyes widened, her stare lifting to meet his. Her words caught deep in her chest, the air sucked out of her lungs. His touch was heated, his fingertips scorching her skin. It was almost too much for her to handle.

As Darryl held her tight, he stood in awe at just how beautiful she was. He couldn't even begin to deny how much he wanted her. Even when she was being quarrelsome, he still found her attractive. There was no denying that the friendship between them had grown into something much more. And in that moment, standing there with his arm around her, all he wanted was to kiss her, to feel his lips pressed tight to hers.

His father's voice calling from the front porch of the family home pulled him from the trance he'd fallen into.

"Darryl! Hey, son!"

Closing his eyes, Darryl took a deep inhale of air. He opened his eyes and met Camryn's stare. Her lips were slightly parted in anticipation. He took another breath and gently caressed her back, his fingers teasing the curve of her buttocks.

"Darryl!"

He took a step back, his hand moving from her back to the car door. He pushed it open as wide as it could go. His gaze moved from her face to where his father stood waving. "Yes, sir?"

"Remember what I said, son," Senior called out. "Be careful!"

Darryl chuckled under his breath, his head waving from side to side. "Yes, sir, Senior!" He dropped his gaze back to Camryn, the two staring at each momentarily.

Smiling brightly, Camryn suddenly drew the back of her fingers down the side of his face. He smiled with her. When she leaned up to press a damp kiss against Darryl's cheek, he felt his heart skip a beat and then two. Mindful of his parents still watching from the porch, Camryn lifted her hand in an easy wave before easing into the car. She pulled the seat belt around her slight frame and latched it as Darryl stood watching her.

"So it's like that?" he said.

Camryn laughed and he couldn't stop himself from laughing with her.

Chapter 9

"He was a great guy but he wanted a pregnant, stay-at-home wife."

"And that wasn't you?" Darryl asked.

Camryn shrugged. "No, not back then. My career has always come before my personal life." She pulled a hand through her hair. "What about you? How long did your *thing* with Pauline Satterwhite last?"

Darryl laughed. "Just long enough for her to take my virginity and leave me wanting. The girl was cold."

"Oh, no, she didn't!"

"Yes, she did," he said.

"And your father remembered her name?"

"Apparently my little secret wasn't so secret," Darryl said, chuckling.

"So, did you think Asia was the one?"

Darryl shifted his eyes from the road to Camryn's face and back again. "Asia thought she was the one.

I cared about her but I probably knew early on that it wasn't going to work out. My mother didn't care for her at all and my sisters detested her with a passion. It's hard to be in love with a woman your mother doesn't like."

"I can't imagine your mother not liking someone."

"Exactly."

Camryn laughed. "So, help me out here—you have four sisters, right?"

"Yes, and five brothers."

"Where do you fall in the lineup?"

"Smack dab in the middle. I'm the fifth child and the third oldest son."

"Wow! Tell me about them."

"We're a family of successful overachievers. Mason is the oldest. He made billions in the hotel industry. Then there's my sister Maitlyn. She freelances as a talent agent but spends most of her time managing all of our lives. My brother Donovan is next and he's a mathematician. If you need the numbers crunched, he's your go-to man.

"Then comes my sister Katrina. She's a district court judge in Texas. And, of course, me, engineer extraordinaire. The twins came after me, Kendrick and Kamaya. I'm not sure what Kendrick does is legal. I just know he's good at it and makes a lot of money. And Kamaya works wonders with roots."

Camryn laughed. "Roots?"

"We're all still trying to figure that out." He laughed. "Then there's my brother Guy, the actor. You would probably recognize him from the James Bond movie."

"*The* Guy Boudreaux? That's your brother?"

"My baby brother! And last but not least, there's my

baby sister, Tarah. She's in medical school, soon to be a heart surgeon."

Camryn shifted in her seat, twisting more toward him. "Your parents must be exceptionally proud of you all."

"They are," Darryl said with a quick nod. "But then, Senior is retired military. He set very high standards for us. But what about you? I know you have a twin brother, right?"

"Yes. He's older by exactly two minutes. Daddy always hoped Carson would work the business with him but after spending a year in France, Carson went to culinary school and opened a chain of restaurants instead."

"Was he disappointed?" He looked at her. "Your father, I mean."

Camryn tossed him an easy smile. "No, not at all. Daddy has always wanted us both to just be happy. Besides, he got me and I'm a better architect than Carson would ever have been." Camryn smiled again.

The two had been talking and driving for a few hours, a slow sojourn into the countryside outside of New Orleans. They'd been heading upriver, following the River Road and the plantation homes that lined the banks of the Mississippi. They'd stopped a few times: two restroom breaks, a late-afternoon lunch and quick excursions into a few antiques shops that had caught Camryn's eye. Before either realized it, they were in the heart of Cajun Country.

"So, where are we going?" Camryn finally asked.

Darryl eased the car through downtown St. Martinville. Maneuvering into a parking space near the city park, he shut off the engine.

"I felt like walking along the Bayou Teche," he said casually as he moved to her side of the car and opened the door.

The waterway meandered through the town, shimmering beneath the late-afternoon sunlight. The sun was beating down hard and a thick patch of humidity had rolled in, making the air murky and sticky, sapping energy from even the most enthusiastic. The streets were shaded by century-old mossy oaks. The views could easily be from a postcard.

Together Camryn and Darryl strolled the concrete walkways, eyeing the birds that waded among cattails, an old man fishing in the stream, a family enjoying a picnic meal in the park. Conversation continued to flow easily between them. Spying an empty bench, Camryn grabbed Darryl's hand and pulled him along beside her, dropping down onto the wooden seat.

"My body is exhausted," she said, blowing a gust of breath. She stretched the length of her limbs out in front of her.

"I know. That's why you needed to take a break. You've been burning the candle at both ends, Ms. Charles."

"Hard work reaps generous rewards, Mr. Boudreaux."

"It does. But all work and no play makes you a royal pain."

Camryn laughed. "I guess I have been a bit difficult lately."

"A bit?" Darryl chuckled. "That's putting it mildly."

"I have not been that bad."

Darryl cut his eyes at her, his eyebrows raised. "If you say so."

"I do," she said, grinning broadly. She took a deep breath and allowed the silence to swell between them. The moment was comfortable, the quiet just shy of being perfection. As Darryl stared out over the landscape, Camryn couldn't help but ask the question she'd been building up her nerves for since they'd left his family home.

"So, do you really talk about me all the time?" she finally inquired.

He smiled, turning to stare at her. Camryn looked off toward the water, feigning disinterest.

"Yeah," he said finally. "I do."

"Why?"

Darryl paused as he considered his response. "Probably because I think about you all the time," he answered.

She tossed him a quick glance. "Really?"

"I think about what a pain in the ass you are!"

Camryn gave him a playful punch. After stretching a second time she leaned her body into the curve of his arm, resting her head against his broad chest as she lifted her legs onto the bench, crossing them at the ankles. There was brief pause before she spoke. "I think about you all the time, too," she said softly.

Darryl was only slightly stunned by her confession. He wrapped both his arms around her torso and shifted closer to her.

She continued. "We shouldn't be thinking about each other at all. It's very unprofessional, Darryl Boudreaux."

His laugh was amiable and teasing and she enjoyed the warmth of his body next to hers, his chest rising and falling against her back as he chuckled. He drew the length of his fingers against her bare arms. The gentle caress caused her nipples to press taut against the fabric of her lace bra. She crossed her arms over her chest, hoping against all odds that Darryl would not notice.

"You won't get any argument from me," Darryl said casually. "I agree with you wholeheartedly. You should not be thinking about me, Camryn Charles."

"We're friends and that's a good thing because we work so well together," Camryn reasoned. "We wouldn't want to do anything that might ruin our working relationship. Right?"

Darryl nodded. He pressed his face into her hair, inhaling the fresh scent of mandarin and orchids against the strands. She smelled divine, the sweet aroma teasing his senses. Currents of electricity tingled through his body. A rise of nature strained heavily through his crotch. He moved his body to cross his legs, hoping to stall the rush of arousal.

He pressed a kiss against the top of Camryn's head, then nuzzled his nose into the curve of her neck. "We definitely wouldn't want to do that," he muttered against her skin as his fingertips trailed lightly over her neck and shoulders.

She leaned into his hand, enjoying the sensation of his touch. Before she realized it, a low moan managed to escape past her lips. Her eyes flew open from the infraction. Darryl smiled down at her, and his eyes softened, desire shimmering in the dark orbs. Staring into them, Camryn felt herself falling, all control lost. She fought to regain some footing. "We have to keep our relationship strictly professional," she whispered, her tone hardly convincing.

Darryl whispered into her ear. "If you say so," he said just before sliding his tongue along the edge of Camryn's earlobe.

Camryn gasped loudly, feeling herself shiver with expectation. "Ohhh! Darryl, you have to stop!"

Suddenly Darryl tapped her lightly against the curve of her hip. "I'm sorry. We should be going," he said as he pushed her gently from him and stood up. "Before I do something we'll both regret."

Moving to her feet, Camryn wrapped her arms tightly around her torso. She took in a deep breath, closing her eyes briefly as she struggled to regain her composure. Darryl had her feeling some kind of way and it was almost too much for her to handle. She lifted her face to the bright sun, allowing the heated rays to gently soothe the unrest brewing inside of her. When she finally opened her eyes, Darryl was staring at her, a pained expression wrinkling his brow. He reached a large hand out to gently stroke the side of her face. Without him having to say a word, Camryn felt exactly what he was feeling and she took a step toward him, moving her body easily against his.

The look she gave him was enchanting, her stare an overflowing fountain of emotion. "I won't regret it," she whispered as she slid her arms around his waist, the soft curves of her body pressing tightly to the hard lines of his. "I won't have any regrets at all," she repeated.

And so he kissed her, his lips connecting with hers ever so sweetly. The world stood still. Their mouths were pressed tightly together, flesh gliding like silk against satin.

He tasted sweet, like chocolate and mint. His hands closed around her head, his fingers entwined in the curls of her hair. His lips were eager, anxiously searching her lips. He licked her mouth lightly, seeking permission to go further. Her mouth opened and her breath was honeyed, her tongue warm and darting. The kiss was long and deep and the moment was intoxicating, both completely lost in it. When they finally pulled away from each other, both panting heavily, Darryl knew that he had no regrets, either. Not a single one.

Chapter 10

Darryl reached for Camryn's hand as they headed back to his car, palms pressed together, arms swinging easily between them. The woman pointed with her free hand and as Darryl turned to look where she indicated, he laughed heartily.

From where Asia sat watching, they looked quite comfortable with each other. She couldn't remember Darryl ever looking that at ease or that happy when they were together. She took a deep breath, wholly unnerved by the reality of her situation.

She'd been following Darryl for almost a week, excited at the prospect of being reunited with him. She'd watched him run from office to office, office to work site, and it was obvious that he'd been committedly focused on business. Today had been the first day that he'd deviated from his normal routine, pleasure seeming to be the agenda for the afternoon.

Since arriving in Louisiana Asia had learned about the partnership between the Boudreaux and Charles families. She knew of the talented architect Camryn Charles. They'd once competed for a project and Camryn had bested her. But Asia's father had eased that sting by giving her another project to work on. Having a parent with a global architectural firm had its perks. As she sat watching Darryl and Camryn together, she couldn't begin to fathom how her father could ever fix the hurt she was feeling.

Sinking down in the driver's seat of her rental car, Asia ducked her head as Darryl pulled out of his parking space and eased his car into the afternoon traffic. Her eyes followed the couple in the rearview mirror, watching how Camryn was leaning her body against his. There was no mistaking that there was something more than business going on between Darryl and Camryn. .

Picking up her cell phone, Asia searched through her recent contacts. Within seconds her father answered on the other end.

"What's wrong, Asia?"

"Hey, Daddy! Why does something have to be wrong?"

"I know you, Asia."

"Well, there is nothing wrong. I just wanted to say hello."

"I'm on a tight schedule, honey, so you need to make it quick. Have you seen Darryl?"

Asia swiped at a tear that had pushed past her lashes. "Darryl is good, Daddy. He's been very sweet to me."

"Well, I'm glad things are working out."

"Daddy, did you hear about his partnership with Charles & Charles Architecture?"

"It's a big project. Of course I heard about it. I wish I'd had an opportunity to bid on it but I heard Darryl's brother wanted to work with a local firm. He's hired one of the best, so I'm sure he'll be pleased with the outcome. The official groundbreaking is tomorrow, right?"

"Tomorrow? Oh, yeah, right. It's tomorrow," Asia responded, her mind suddenly racing.

"Well, please give Darryl my regards. And, Asia, try to stay out of trouble!"

"I love you, Daddy!"

"I love you, too, Asia."

Disconnecting the call, Asia started the ignition and turned her car back toward New Orleans. She had to prepare for tomorrow.

Darryl stepped into the heated spray of his morning shower, relishing the warm downpour of water that rained down over his head. He pressed both hands against the tiled wall, pushing back just enough to stretch the last remnants of sleep out of his back and shoulders as the stainless-steel showerhead pelted water over his muscular body.

Maneuvering the shower's massage feature, he adjusted the spray until the pressurized water was kneading the last kink out of his body. He tilted his head back so that the water hit him in the chest with full force and then swiped his palm across his face and head, twisting his neck from side to side.

Steam filled the enclosed space, painting the tile and walls with a fine mist. It felt good and necessary and

Darryl languished in the moment. He took a deep breath and then another, fighting the sluggishness that didn't seem to want to leave him.

He'd had a restless night, sleep eluding him for most of it as he'd tossed and turned. The previous day had been one of the best he'd ever had. His connection with Camryn had shifted and it felt good to feel so close to her. Despite his best efforts to ignore his attraction to her, he found himself completely enamored. He liked Camryn more than he'd been willing to admit and there was no denying that there was something special between them.

The kiss they shared had moved his spirit. Camryn's touch was like nothing he'd ever experienced. She made him feel good and when they were together, everything seemed right with the world. Just thinking about her had him grinning from ear to ear and had lengthened an erection, the wealth of his manhood stretched against his body for attention. He clasped his hand around his rock-hard member and gently stroked the firm flesh, wishing it was Camryn's hand and not his own wrapped around his appendage.

Their ride back had been uneventful. They'd chatted casually, feeling no need to comment on the kiss they'd shared or the desire that was surging between them. What they wanted from each other remained unspoken but clearly understood. They felt it in each other's touch, in the way they looked at one another, by the ease of their conversations.

As they'd gotten closer to New Orleans, Camryn had fallen asleep. Her head had rested against his shoulder, an arm draped across his lap. He'd blown a gentle kiss against her forehead and had let her sleep, knowing that she hadn't rested well in weeks. With everything she had riding on the success of Boudreaux Towers, Camryn had been giving every minute of her time to working and working hard. A good night's sleep had become a precious commodity.

By the time they'd reached her front door it had been late. Camryn had invited him inside, her eyes making promises that he would have given anything to partake in if only it were the right moment. But knowing the day that lay ahead for them, he'd resisted, promising a rain check. The look in her eyes had shifted to disappointment and although she'd said she understood, Darryl knew that that was the last thing either of them had wanted. He shook his head, still questioning what had held him back. He'd been fantasizing about making love to Camryn for weeks and when the opportunity presented itself, he'd resisted.

Reaching for a washrag and a bar of Ivory soap, he lathered his torso, suds rolling over his dark complexion down to the drain beneath his feet. Adjusting the temperature on the water flow, he reveled in the warmth, soaping himself once, twice and then a third time before stepping out of the shower and wrapping a plush white towel around his solid frame.

As Darryl dried the moisture from his skin, he tossed the day's agenda around in his mind. The groundbreaking ceremony had been Camryn's idea, part of the promotional campaign to engage the community and neighborhood in the project. Darryl had ensured there was much publicity about the event, inviting every media outlet in the state. Most if not all of the Bou-

dreaux family was scheduled to be there, excited to be
able to celebrate Mason's dream and Darryl's accom-
plishment. They even anticipated the mayor of New Orleans being there to help with the honors. There would
be hours of schmoozing with the press, multiple photo
opportunities, lunch with the town council and various
civic groups, and at some point a meeting with Mason
and Kenneth Charles to update them on the schedule
for the next six months.

His thoughts returned to Camryn and getting some
quality alone time with the beauty. He wanted desperately to make that happen soon.

Camryn couldn't believe she'd overslept, rising an
hour later than she'd planned. She had hoped to stop
by her office for one last review before heading over
to the construction site for the official groundbreaking
ceremony. Realizing that wasn't going to happen, she
tried to shift gears.

Standing in front of the full-length mirror that
adorned her bedroom wall, she shifted one foot and
then the other, still undecided about which pair of shoes
to wear with her Rachel Roy silk caftan blouse and sten-
ciled skirt. She was leaning toward the nude Christian
Louboutin high heel, but there was something equally
charming about the Manolo Blahnik patent leather.
Camryn loved a beautiful shoe and with a few hundred pairs in her closet to select from, making a decision was always a challenge. Still, choosing a shoe
should not have been a big deal but Camryn couldn't
focus. Despite the hectic schedule ahead of her, all she
could think about was Darryl.

Darryl Boudreaux had made her completely lose her mind. The man had her imagining all kinds of things that involved him and her in very wicked, sensuous, possibly compromising positions. She suddenly broke out in a sweat. Rushing to the bathroom, she swiped a damp towel over her face, snaking it down into her bra and beneath her shirt. Getting through this day was going to be difficult at best, Camryn mused.

She stared at her reflection in the large ornate vanity mirror. Darryl had told her she was beautiful, whispering into her ear when he'd thought she'd already dozed off. He'd nuzzled her gently, his feathery touch like a whisper against her skin. And then there had been the kiss. There weren't enough poetic words in the English language to describe his kiss. Camryn bit down against her bottom lip at the memory, a wave of heat washing over her body.

She'd been more than ready to open herself up to him when they'd arrived back at her home, but Darryl had turned down her invitation, reminding her of the day ahead and intoning that she needed to get some rest. He'd been the perfect gentleman and all Camryn had wanted him to do was strip them both naked and make love to her.

Darryl had left her wanting and needy and just when she'd considered questioning his intentions, he'd pulled her close, murmuring in her ear. "I can't wait to get you naked but I want it to be perfect." Then he'd kissed her cheek and ushered her inside her home.

Remembering that she had a job to do, she took a quick glance at the watch on her wrist, rushed back into her bedroom, kicked off her heels and quickly pulled on a pair of black riding boots. After one last check of her makeup she grabbed her leather attaché and headed for the door.

Seconds later the entire neighborhood could hear Camryn's screams. "No, no, no!" she cried, throwing her purse and briefcase to the ground as she surveyed four perfectly flattened tires. Her car sat in the driveway on bare rims. Circling the vehicle in one direction and then back in the other, Camryn shook her head as she inspected the damage. All four tires had been slashed, necessitating much more than a pump of air. Of all days for her to have to deal with vandalism, this was not the morning. Camryn moved back to pick up her bags. She frantically dug through the bottom of her purse searching for her cell phone.

And then she remembered, she had left it in Darryl's car the night before.

Chapter 11

Kenneth Charles gestured for Darryl's attention. Darryl was in deep conversation with the mayor of New Orleans, the newly elected official bending his ear about his plans for the city's economic rejuvenation. With a nod of his head, Darryl politely excused himself from the conversation and followed Mr. Charles away from the crowd.

"Darryl, do you have a clue where my daughter might be?" the older man asked.

Darryl shook his head. "No, sir. I was expecting her to be one of the first people here. I was going to try to call her but the mayor—"

Kenneth waved his hand dismissively. "I've tried to call her a few times and I haven't got an answer."

A look of concern crossed Darryl's face. "Why don't I go see if I can find her?"

"No, I'll send my son. One of you needs to be here

for the ceremony, so we definitely can't have you disappearing anywhere." The older man glanced at his Rolex. "No matter what, we need to get started in the next fifteen minutes. Camryn knows how I feel about punctuality."

Kenneth dialed on his cell phone, shaking his head when there was still no answer from his daughter. He dialed a second number and when Carson Charles answered, Kenneth bellowed into the receiver. "Carson, son, where are you? I need you to swing by Camryn's house. That girl should have been here by now!"

As he waited for Kenneth to complete his call, Darryl eyeballed the growing crowd. He noticed his parents coming through the entrance, Mason leading the way. Lifting his hand to wave, he stopped short when he saw Asia Landry slip into the line behind his sisters. The color immediately drained from his face.

"I need to go find Camryn," he said abruptly, cutting off Kenneth's conversation. "I need to go now," he muttered as he hurried toward the opposite gate, ignoring the contractor trying to point him in the other direction.

Scurrying past the heavy equipment, he raced to his car. Darryl couldn't begin to fathom why Asia was there but he instinctively knew that it had something to do with Camryn *not* being there.

As he fumbled with his car keys, struggling to get the door open, a yellow cab pulled up beside him. The driver gestured out the window, tossing him a quick wave of his hand. A wave of relief washed over him when Camryn jumped from the backseat.

"Please have some cash on you," she gushed, her warm smile greeting him.

"Are you okay?" Darryl questioned. "I was just about to go look for you."

"I woke up late. Then I had four flat tires and I couldn't find my cell phone. I knocked on half the doors in the neighborhood before someone answered and called me a cab. But I'm here. I just need some cash, please."

Darryl reached into the breast pocket of his suit jacket and pulled out his billfold. The driver thanked him profusely when Darryl added a twenty-dollar tip to the fare. As the taxi pulled away, Darryl moved to Camryn's side and pulled her into his arms. Dropping his mouth to hers, he captured her lips beneath his own, his kiss possessive and demanding. When he finally let her mouth go, he pressed the side of his cheek to her cheek. "I was worried about you."

Wrapped in his arms, Camryn felt safe and protected, every anxiety that had plagued her morning dissipating into thin air. His concern was comforting and despite her earlier frustrations, she couldn't have been happier. She hugged him warmly, her palms pressed against his back. They held on to each for a good length of time, both oblivious to everything else around them.

"My father is probably having a fit right about now," she said when she finally pulled away. "He doesn't believe in being late for anything."

"He's been worried, too," Darryl said as he clasped her hand beneath his and pulled her along beside him.

Kenneth stood waiting at the entrance. "Where have you been, Camryn?" he queried, annoyance tingeing his expression.

"I apologize, Father! Some kids vandalized my car. I didn't anticipate having to find a ride this morning."

"Why didn't you call?"

"I couldn't find my cell phone. I'm pretty sure I dropped it in Darryl's car yesterday."

Kenneth shook his head. "I don't understand why you kids have forsaken a good house phone for your cell phones. It does not make an ounce of sense to me. It's not like you can't afford the bill. Hell, I'll pay the damn bill!"

"It's a waste of money, Father, but after today I might have to give it some consideration."

After a deep sigh, Kenneth leaned to kiss his daughter's cheek. "Well, I'm glad you're here. I'll call your brother and tell him to deal with your car. Darryl, I'm going to entrust my daughter to you. Make sure she gets home safely tonight, please."

Darryl smiled, lifting his gaze to meet Camryn's. "Not a problem, sir."

"Did you see your brother?" Katherine Boudreaux asked as Mason guided the family toward the reserved seating area.

"He's here somewhere," Mason said, pulling out a seat for his mother. "We'll be starting any minute now, so he better be!"

As Mason turned to indicate the seating for his sisters, he was taken aback to see Asia Landry standing at the edge of the aisle. "Mason, hello!" the woman called nervously. "How is everyone?" she said, waving her hand in the family's direction.

"Asia…hello," Katherine said with hesitance.

Darryl's father gave her a quick nod of his head.

"What are you doing here?" Tarah Boudreaux asked, voicing what everyone else was thinking.

"I came to support Darryl," Asia said matter-of-factly, a syrupy grin pulling at her thin lips.

"Did he invite you?" Kamaya Boudreaux asked. "Because I highly doubt my brother would invite you!"

"I hope they made you go through a metal detector," Tarah added.

Katherine held up her hand, stalling her daughters' attitudes. "We're all here to support Darryl and Mason, so there will be no showing out. Is that understood?" Katherine tossed both of her daughters a look.

Tarah nodded.

"Yes, ma'am," Kamaya mumbled.

"Is that understood, Asia?" Katherine repeated.

"I wouldn't think of causing a scene, Mama Boudreaux," Asia chimed.

With a raised brow, Katherine gave Asia a look. An awkward silence fell over the group. Kamaya and Tarah cut their eyes at one another as their brother fought not to laugh out loud. Senior rolled his eyes skyward. He met Mason's stare and held it, the two men having a silent conversation between them.

Mason took a deep breath. "Asia, I apologize but I wasn't aware that you would be here. There's only enough seating here for the immediate family. Why don't you come with me so we can find you a comfortable seat where you'll have a great view."

"Oh…oh…" Asia stammered. "I'm sorry. I don't know what I was thinking! Of course, Mason! I guess it would ruin the surprise if Darryl saw me in the front row," she said with a nervous giggle.

"And we don't want to spoil the surprise," Mason said as he clutched her elbow and led her away.

"Can you believe the audacity!" Tarah exclaimed when the two were out of earshot.

"That girl needs her ass whopped," Kamaya started.

"Mind your mouth," Senior interrupted, his tone scolding.

"Darryl's going to be surprised, all right," Kendrick noted.

"Unfortunately, I think Asia is the one in for a surprise," Katherine said, gesturing toward the gate where Darryl and Camryn were making their way through the entrance. The family all turned to watch as he placed a kiss on Camryn's lips.

"Awww, sookie-sookie now!" Kendrick chuckled.

"This is going to be good!" Kamaya interjected, grinning broadly. She turned to her twin to get a high five.

Katherine shook her head. "Lord, have mercy!" she muttered softly.

Across the way, Mason settled Asia in a seat next to the local dignitaries. Glancing back to his family, he moved toward the side gate where Darryl, Camryn and Kenneth stood in conversation.

"Camryn, you made it," Mason chimed as he leaned to kiss the young woman's cheek.

"I did, Mason, and I apologize for the delay."

"It's a long story," Darryl interjected, meeting his brother's eyes.

"And interesting, I'm sure," Mason said. The two

men exchanged looks as Mason shifted his gaze past Darryl's shoulder to where Asia sat. Darryl's stare followed where his brother was looking and he nodded his acknowledgment.

Camryn looked from one to the other, sensing something was going on that she didn't understand. She tossed Darryl a curious look and just as she was about to ask them what they were being so secretive about, her father interrupted.

"Well, are we all ready?" Kenneth asked.

"Yes, sir," Darryl answered. "I think we're more than ready."

The ceremony was over quickly. The speeches were short and sweet and after Mason and Kenneth both extended gratitude to half the city of New Orleans and each other, Darryl passed a gold-toned shovel to the mayor, who pretended to dig into the rich soil. The photo opportunities with everyone and that shovel took longer than the speeches. Shortly after, family and friends rushed to extend their congratulations.

After posing for a photograph with her father, Camryn fielded questions from a local newspaper. Out of the corner of her eye she noticed the attractive woman pulling at Darryl's elbow for attention. It was the harsh expression that briefly crossed his face that she found unnerving. Darryl and the woman were engaged in deep conversation until they were interrupted by Darryl's family. The exchange seemed heated at best despite Darryl's efforts to look unconcerned. Darryl was a man who wore his emotions on his sleeve, so there was no mistaking that he was not a happy camper.

The woman was familiar but Camryn could not place

where she knew her from. She was petite in stature with hips for days. Her shortly cropped hairstyle was complementary to her round face. Her makeup was just a touch too heavy for Camryn's taste but her dress was stylish and flattering to her figure and she had on a killer pair of five-inch designer heels. But there was something about the way she kept grabbing Darryl's arm that set Camryn's nerves on edge.

After satisfying the reporter's last question, Camryn eased her way over to join the group.

"Mr. and Mrs. Boudreaux, it's a pleasure to see you again," she said, greeting Darryl's parents warmly.

Senior pumped her arm excitedly. "Nice job, young lady. Very nice job. You and Darryl should be very proud of yourselves."

She smiled brightly. "Darryl and I make a great team," she said.

Senior laughed. "Sounds like the honeymoon's back on," he teased.

Camryn extended her hand to Darryl's brother. "Hello! I'm Camryn Charles," she said as she introduced herself.

Darryl shook Asia off his arm and moved to Camryn's side. "Camryn, I'm sorry. This is my brother Kendrick and my sisters Kamaya and Tarah. Everyone, this is our star architect, Camryn Charles."

"It's going to be a beautiful building," Tarah said as she and Camryn shared a casual hug. "It must be very exciting."

"It is," Camryn said with a nod. "I'm so glad you all could make it."

"We're still missing a few," Katherine intoned, "but

I'm sure you'll meet the rest of the Boudreaux bunch sometime soon."

Pushing her way to the front of the line, Asia extended a hand in Camryn's direction. "Camryn Charles! I'm Asia Landry and it's a pleasure to meet you."

Camryn's eyes widened in surprise. "My goodness! Asia, it's a pleasure to meet you, too. I've heard a lot about you."

Asia chuckled. "Don't believe it all!"

"Well, I loved your work on the Markum project in Chicago. You have a wonderful design aesthetic."

"I appreciate that. I'm equally impressed with your work. And it looks like you and Darryl will be outdoing yourselves with this project."

Camryn smiled, skirting her eyes in Darryl's direction. "Thank you."

Asia stepped in closer. "So," she said, her gaze sweeping from the top of Camryn's head down to the tips of her boots and back. "Are you and Darryl good friends?"

"Excuse me?"

"You and Darryl. Is there something going on between you two?" Asia demanded, her tone suddenly antagonistic. "Because I don't take kindly to other women pressing up on my man."

"Asia!" Darryl snapped.

"I meant what I said about not showing out," Katherine interjected.

Asia took another step closer to Camryn, her voice raised. "Are you and Darryl sleeping together?"

There was another awkward silence, Darryl's family shooting glances around the area to see who might have been listening.

Darryl called her name again. "Asia, that's enough!"

Camryn threw Darryl an uneasy look, her head moving slightly from side to side. She took a deep breath and slowly blew it out. She took the next step, meeting Asia toe to toe. "Not until the wedding," she said smugly.

Shock registered on Asia's face. "What wedding?"

"You didn't hear?" Camryn responded.

"No!"

The other woman shrugged. "Well, it was on a need-to-know basis and I guess everyone figured you didn't need to know anything about what goes on with me and Darryl."

Kendrick burst out laughing. Tarah fought to stifle her own giggles.

"Oh, yeah! I like her." Kamaya signified.

Asia bristled, her face skewing into all facets of ugly.

"Asia, you really need to leave, please," Darryl said. He gently rested his palm against the curve of her arm. "Before I call the police and have you escorted out. That restraining order is still in effect."

Snatching her arm from his touch, Asia turned an about-face. "I just came to support you," she snarled. "And this is the thanks I get?"

"Little girl, it's time for you to go," Senior said, stepping between the two women. "Do you need someone to give you a ride?"

Kendrick moved to his father's side, his eyes locked on Asia.

She turned her gaze back to Darryl. "I can't believe you'd let these people treat me like this. You know I love you."

Darryl shook his head. "You need to take your meds,

Asia," he said softly. "And you need to leave. This is not the time or the place for this conversation."

"Tch!" Asia sucked her teeth. Her gaze swept around the faces staring at her as if she was crazy. A half snarl painted her expression.

"My father sends you all his best regards," Asia finally said, and with that she spun around on her high heels and stormed back through the gated entrance.

As Asia stomped away, Senior shook his head and cleared his throat. He met Darryl's anxious stare. "On that note, I think it's time we all went and got us some lunch!" Reaching out for his wife's hand, he led the way, the family following.

Darryl reached out to wrap his arms around Camryn's shoulders. He locked eyes with her. "Sorry about that," he said, his voice a whisper.

Camryn shrugged. "Don't be. It's not your fault," she said as they both turned to catch up to their families. But there was something in her voice that didn't sound convincing.

Darryl took one last look over his shoulder. His father's words echoed in his head. He still had some unfinished business that needed to be handled.

"Those two seem to be getting along famously," Camryn said, nodding her head toward Darryl's father and her own, who were standing in the adjacent room.

"They're both cut from the same cloth," Darryl answered, turning to stare where she stared.

The two men had been engaged in deep conversation for most of the afternoon, huddled in a corner of the Charles family home. Most of the afternoon had been a lecture-fest from the senior members of the two families. Senior had lectured them. Kenneth had lectured them. Katherine had lectured them and even Mason had tossed in two cents. By the time all the lecturing was done and finished, the day was almost gone.

"You look tired," Darryl said, tracing the profile of Camryn's face with his index finger.

"It's been a very long day."

"Well, if you're ready, I can take you home."

Camryn smiled. "Actually, Darryl, I think I'm going to stay here with my father tonight."

There was a moment of pause. "Why?" Darryl asked.

Camryn wrapped her arms tightly around her torso. "I just do."

Darryl nodded. "Are you upset about Asia?"

She shrugged her narrow shoulders, jutting them skyward. "I think I just have some issues I need to resolve." There was a hint of attitude in her tone.

"Issues between us? Because if you have an issue with *us,* or with *me,* then we need to resolve it together."

"Is there an *us?* I thought *we* were just friends."

"Just until the wedding," Darryl said casually, crossing his own arms across his chest.

Camryn shot him a look, her eyes narrowing into thin slits.

"Don't look at me like that," Darryl said with a deep chuckle. "You went there first."

"She asked for it."

He nodded slowly, a pregnant pause filling the space between them. Darryl broke the silence. "Camryn, we're more than friends and you know it."

She took a deep breath. "Darryl, right now all I know

is that your girlfriend more than likely slashed my tires. She definitely caused a scene in front of my father, your family and our business associates. And I would venture to guess that she's not done. I have to worry about what might come next."

"She is not my girlfriend."

"Are you sure about that? Because she thinks she's your girlfriend and I'm just a woman pushing up on you."

"You're only pushing up on me until the honeymoon."

"You're not funny, Darryl."

Darryl reached out and wrapped his arms around her waist and pulled her to him. She clutched the front of his shirt as her body curved easily against his. She lifted her eyes to his, the stare he was giving her consuming her as his gaze skated over her face. Camryn fought to catch her breath.

"No, I'm not being funny. I'm very serious." Darryl's face reflected the rush of emotion overwhelming his spirit. She could see him mulling over his next words, choosing them carefully. "I never had a best friend before…until you. And for the last few months I think you and I have become best friends. And I think you feel the same way about me. I would venture to say that you want to move this relationship forward as much as I do, Camryn."

She nodded her head. "But what about Asia? I'll be honest. The woman is a little unhinged. You know what she did to my car. What might she do to my home, or me?"

"What about her? Asia has problems that have nothing to do with me, or you. She's not my girlfriend and she and I are definitely not friends. She's my past and I assure you I am not looking behind me. Now, I regret what happened today. And I apologize that Asia brought her drama to our event but I didn't have any control over that. What I have control over is what I do. And right now what I want to do is be with you. I want to make love to you. I want to wake up with you. I want to fight with you. I want to laugh with you. I want to breathe your air, Camryn. Do you get that? I have been thinking about *us* and *us* being together since the first day I laid eyes on you. And if you're going to make me wait until the wedding, then we're headed to the justice of the peace right now. Because I have fallen in love with you, Camryn."

"Darryl, I…I… We…" she stammered, at a complete loss for words.

Darryl tightened his grip on her. "Say it! Say what you need to say."

Camryn took a deep breath, her eyes misting lightly with tears. "I think I love you, too," she said, her voice a loud whisper.

Darryl grinned. "I don't *think* you do. I *know* you do."

Camryn giggled. "You ain't all that!" she said teasingly.

Standing in his arms, Camryn suddenly felt as though there wasn't anything the two of them couldn't get through together. He was her best friend and he had her heart as no one else ever had.

She reached up to kiss him, her lips hungrily searching out his. There was nothing but love in his kiss. He

have
er price
ne U.S.
anada, bu
FREE!
en send you
onderful
ise gifts.
u can't lose!

S!

FREE

miss out—

visit us online at
www.ReaderService.co

loved her. She could taste it, smell it, hear it and feel it. It was like a morning sunrise in a clear blue sky and a full moon on a dark night. It was everything Darryl held sacred and in his arms Camryn couldn't deny it. She loved him, too.

Across the room, Senior and Kenneth both smiled, the two patriarchs exchanging glances. From where she sat on the sofa, Katherine tossed the two men an all-knowing look. Standing in the doorway, Kamaya, Kendrick and Camryn's brother, Carson, all burst out laughing.

Kendrick shook his head, leaning on Carson's shoulder. "I want to breathe your air!" the two men chimed in unison. Mimicking Darryl and Camryn, they sent the whole room into a fit of laughter.

But just feet away, Darryl and Camryn stood wrapped in each other's arms, completely oblivious to their families' banter.

Chapter 12

Knowing that Camryn had reservations about returning to her home, Darryl rented the penthouse suite at the
Omni Hotel on St. Louis Street. It was eight hundred
fifty square feet of luxury accommodations tastefully
furnished in nineteenth-century New Orleans decor.
The foyer led to a living area with French doors that
overlooked the French Quarter, a private balcony, a wet
bar and a dining area. The bathrooms were marbled and
the master bedroom included an oversize Jacuzzi tub
and double walk-in shower.

Nervous didn't begin to describe the wealth of emotion that he was feeling. Darryl opened the suite door
and led her down the hallway into the living space.
At one point he turned and walked backward, watching her. She was weak-kneed, trying to walk steady
on her heels. His gaze roamed the length of her legs,
then up her body to her face. He sucked on his bottom

lip and his tongue pushed slightly past his lips as he licked them. There was a look of longing in his eyes and Camryn couldn't remember the last time she had felt so wanted.

Standing before the large mirror in the bedroom, Camryn rested her palms on the dresser as she stepped out of her shoes. She took off one diamond earring and then the other, resting the studs against the dresser top. Darryl eased himself behind her, leaning his body against hers. He was warm against her back and Camryn attempted to control her excitement.

Darryl's hands dropped to her hips, and then glided slowly across her abdomen. He pressed his pelvis against the curve of her buttocks, pulling her closer to him. When he leaned to press his lips against her neck, kissing her gently, she purred ever so softly. Camryn pushed her behind backward into Darryl's crotch and he responded by moving his hands to the zipper of her skirt. He undid the button and pulled the zipper down slowly. Camryn quivered with anticipation, nothing but sheer will keeping her standing upright. She grabbed the dresser with both hands, leaning forward as Darryl eased her skirt off her hips and pushed them down to her ankles. She stepped out of it and then turned to face him.

Gripping her by her buttocks, Darryl pulled her against him, kissing her hungrily. A rock-hard erection pressed against her pelvic bone. Darryl ground himself against her, the sensation shooting heat through every fiber of his being. He met her stare, her eyes glazed with desire. Her gaze locked with his and she smiled, her lips parting ever so slightly. She turned back toward the mirror, looking into his eyes in the glass. She licked her lips as she pulled her sweater up over her head and Darryl felt as though he were about to combust, every hardened muscle feeling as if it were about to explode.

Darryl's hands danced over her black laced bra. He unhooked it in the back and pushed the straps off her shoulders, the garment falling slowly from her body. His hands were hot, his touch dropping bursts of heat across her skin. She had beautiful breasts, full and high, with protruding nipples that were almost as large as her thumb and defined by perfect areolas the color of dark chocolate.

He palmed them both at the same time and her nipples bubbled full and hard beneath his fingertips. Spinning in his arms, Camryn leaned her body against his as she lifted her face up to kiss him passionately. Their tongues danced together, a sweet two-step. He continued to kiss and caress her and then she licked the roof of his mouth, her hands moving wildly over his body through his clothes.

Lifting her off of her feet, Darryl carried her to the bed, his mouth still connected to hers. Heat danced in large swells around them. Camryn was slightly startled when Darryl suddenly hurled her backward, sending her sprawling to the bed. She gasped loudly as her body bounced easily against the mattress. She watched as he stood above her, staring, nothing but pure, unadulterated lust seeping from his eyes.

Darryl slowly unbuttoned his white dress shirt and slid it from his torso. His muscles bulged, the sinewy lines stretching like taut fiber over hard stone. He unbuckled his pants and pushed them to the floor, stepping out of his slacks and his briefs. His manhood protruded between his legs, his erection long and dark. Camryn leaned up on her elbows feeling like a snake charmer who'd just charmed a mighty snake. She smiled, the seductive gesture triggering Darryl's serpent to twitch and pulse.

He lifted her foot, his fingers gliding across each toe, over the arch, past the heel and around to her ankle. His lips followed where his hands led. He kissed up the length of one leg, down the length of the other and back again. He slipped two fingers beneath the line of her lace thong, the nubs tapping gently at her most private place. Camryn fell back against the bedding as she murmured his name.

"Mmm, Darryl!"

He suddenly snatched the fabric from her body, the garment tearing. Camryn gasped as he tossed it to the floor. He pushed her legs farther apart as he eased himself up between them. She was clean shaven, the skin smooth as silk. He trailed the back of his hand across her groin. She was damp, moisture coating his fingers as he rubbed her wantonly. His fingertips spread her feminine lips apart, parting the delicate folds. Camryn opened herself even more to his touch.

Rising up and over her, he lowered his body down against hers, capturing her mouth again with his own. He tasted her lips, gently sucked on her bottom lip and then her top lip before sliding his tongue against her tongue, savoring the salt and sweet of her. His right hand was still trapped between her legs and he slid two fingers deeply and smoothly inside of her, wiggling them around in slow, steady circles. Camryn threw her head back with pleasure, the infraction leaving her weak and wanting more.

Camryn savored the sensations of his touch, his mouth heating every square inch of skin. He sucked on her earlobe, kissed the spot beneath her chin and licked his way down to her clavicle. He sucked one hard nipple and then the other, drawing each between his lips. He suckled her greedily, kneading the fullness of her breasts with a heavy hand.

Camryn's small hands skated across his broad chest and up over his back. When she reached between them, her hands gliding over his hard abs to touch him as intimately as he touched her, Darryl stopped her. He grabbed her wrists and drew her arms up and over her head. Leaning above her, he shook his head slowly, a wry smile pulling at his mouth. He waved his index finger at her, the appendage skirting from side to side.

"Tonight is all about you," Darryl whispered. "Just you, baby!"

"Mmm," Camryn purred as Darryl resumed his expedition down her body, pausing to worship at her belly button. He dipped his tongue into the crevice. Camryn gasped loudly when he reached for a pillow, lifted her buttocks, and propped it beneath her bottom. He spread her open and Camryn shivered, the mere thought of the intimate kiss curling her toes.

Darryl buried his head between Camryn's thighs. He began to lick her slowly and easily. He teased her clit with the tip of his tongue and she placed a hand on his head, drawing him closer. Her moans were low and quiet as he swirled his tongue in little circles over the swollen nub. She cried out with sheer pleasure when he cupped his tongue to draw it into his mouth. At the same time he penetrated her with one finger and then a second, slowly plunging his hand in and out of her. His tongue continued to lash over her clit, sucking and licking, warm breaths of air blowing on her between licks. With each flick he could feel her body twitch and squirm as he lapped at her with the flat of his tongue. Camryn could feel her secret treasure becoming wetter and wetter, her sweet nectar dripping down onto his bottom lip. The taste of her was driving him crazy and his tongue moved harder and faster as his fingers struggled to keep pace, penetrating her deeper and deeper. And then her muscles clenched and tightened and she spasmed and gushed, filling his mouth with the sweetest honey as she screamed his name over and over again.

The intensity of her orgasm left Camryn panting heavily. Her body had never felt more relaxed as Darryl kissed his way back up her torso. With each touch and caress, her nerve endings fired, every juncture igniting into a mini explosion. It all felt too, too good, Camryn thought as she began to pump her hips up and against his body. As he suckled her neck, Camryn pressed her body up into his, thrusting her pelvis against him.

"I want to feel you inside me," she whispered as she lifted her legs and wrapped them tightly around his naked backside. "I need you inside me, Darryl!" she cooed.

Reaching for a condom he'd laid on the nightstand, he sheathed himself quickly, stretching the length of the prophylactic over his throbbing member. He hovered above her briefly, staring into her eyes. His look was pure gold, every fiber of his being engaged in the moment. He entered her slowly, savoring the sensation of each fold welcoming him into her secret space, her inner lining stretching to accommodate him.

He teased and stroked her, gliding his body in and out of her body, large swells of heat washing over them. Camryn basked in the love that washed over her, Darryl's expression nothing but a wealth of affection looking down on her. Tears misted his eyes as he gave in to the sensations sweeping through his body as he pushed and pulled and pushed himself in and out of her. The pleasure was immeasurable. As Camryn screamed his name, her nails grazed the length of his back. When she exploded, Darryl crashed with her, his own orgasm colliding with hers as they both fell off the edge of ecstasy together.

Darryl's cell phone vibrating against the nightstand pulled Camryn from a deep sleep. She was tempted to see who was calling him but didn't. Snooping was no way to start a relationship and Camryn had learned early on that a man she couldn't trust wasn't a man she wanted to spend her life with.

Darryl slept soundly, snoring ever so softly. Camryn sat upright in the bed. She trailed a hand over his head and across his shoulders and he responded by rolling his body closer to hers as he threw an arm across her lap. Smiling, Camryn cuddled her body to his, relishing the warmth of his body heat.

He smiled in his sleep and Camryn was overjoyed with the expression on his face. If she were a betting woman, she would have speculated that Darryl was dreaming about her. It was a thought she enjoyed imagining. Darryl suddenly rolled over in his sleep, his body sprawling across the mattress. He tossed and kicked the sheet to the floor, exposing his nakedness. Camryn's eyes widened as she surveyed the definition of muscle. The man was fine as hell, hard-bodied with a rich complexion that made her think of decadent chocolates.

Easing down the length of his body, she lightly trailed her fingers over his chest, teasing the fine hairs around his belly button, pausing just above the line of his pubic hair. His flaccid penis twitched ever so slightly. Camryn scooted closer, taking great pains to not wake him from the sleep that had full claim over him. She wrapped her palm around his manhood, the weight of him warm in her hand. He stirred ever so slightly as she gently explored the treasure with her hand. She traced a finger across a large vein that pulsed with his heartbeat, trailing the pad of her finger to the tip and back again.

She loved the feel of the firm stalk in her hand and the amazingly soft skin on the head as she leaned and pressed it to her cheeks and lips. His scent was an intoxicating combination of male musk and the floral scented soap in the hotel's bathroom and it monopolized her senses. The aroma overwhelmed her as she gently inhaled him. All of her nerve endings were suddenly firing, familiar sensations returning as the pheromones teased her. As she continued to gently explore and stroke him, he swelled easily, the fullness of him becoming overinflated. Darryl's manhood throbbed in exquisite pain and he woke feeling as if he were about to burst.

Darryl's heart pounded as Camryn took him into her

mouth, her taste buds awash with his nectar. The massive head felt comfortable in her mouth and she maximized the contact between herself and the soft skin atop his magnificent sex organ. She could feel him begin to thrust into her mouth and she limited his penetration with a tight grip on his shaft. Darryl marveled as she allowed him entry, with each successive thrust aiming for the back of her throat.

Undaunted, Camryn pressed on, taking him slow and easy. She felt him swell and pulse and she eased up on her ministrations when she felt his orgasm approaching. She paused, nothing moving as she let him catch his breath, the stretch to his organ subsiding slowly. Darryl was clearly enjoying her patience and attention to giving him pleasure. He pushed his hips up and down and when she felt him getting hyperexcited again, she took him out of her mouth and swirled her tongue at his tip. Darryl was in awe that Camryn was enjoying the act as much as he was.

The woman didn't miss a trick as she returned his member to her mouth and worked it vigorously with her tongue while pumping his hard shaft with both her hands. It was only seconds before he was swollen to full capacity again, thrusting harder. She heard him moan loudly in anticipation of his climax. And then a final thrust forward, and a loud grunt made Camryn smile at what she had done.

She continued to slowly lick and stroke him as his size gradually diminished and he shriveled back to a state of normality. All of her pleasure centers were alive and she was buzzed, feeling skilled and accomplished. Darryl lifted his head slightly to stare down at her. He waved his head from side to side as she grinned broadly. Reaching for the blankets that had fallen to the floor, Camryn nuzzled back against him, curling her body against his. Drawing his fingers through her hair, Darryl laid back and closed his eyes. Within minutes he was sound asleep and when he awoke the next morning, Camryn was pleasuring him all over again.

Chapter 13

It had been a whole week since Camryn had seen the inside of her home. She and Darryl had spent their nights in the hotel, leaving only to fulfill their respective duties for Boudreaux Enterprises and Charles & Charles Architecture. Every other waking minute was spent exploring each other. By the end of the week they were both exhausted.

"We have to go home," Camryn insisted as Darryl maneuvered his car in the direction of her house. "You can stay with me there."

"My mother has called twice to ask when I'd be back," Darryl responded. "She might overlook my absence for this week, but I'm sure she and Senior both will have something to say if I'm suddenly shacking up with you at your house. So when are we going to have that wedding?" He smiled.

Camryn laughed. "If that's a proposal, Darryl Boudreaux, you need to do better. What kind of girl do you take me for?"

Darryl cut his eye at her, a wide grin across his face. "I take you for my girl, Camryn Charles. Mine and mine alone," he said as he pulled into her driveway.

Camryn shook her head. As they exited the car, a concerned look fell over her face.

"What's wrong?" Darryl questioned.

She shook her head. "The security lights didn't come on," she said. "Usually a breeze will make the motion-sensor lights come on."

"Give me your keys," Darryl said, gesturing for her to place the key ring into his hand.

She followed him to the entrance, moving behind him as he opened the front door and stepped inside. Reaching around him toward the wall, she flicked the light switch. The room remained dark, nothing happening as she flicked the switch multiple times. "That's odd," Camryn said.

"Stay here," Darryl commanded.

"Like hell I will," Camryn responded, grabbing the back of his shirt.

Darryl walked slowly into the home, the interior dark with the exception of the faint moonlight shimmering through the open blinds of her windows. He engaged his cell phone, using the LED light to guide them. Camryn suddenly tugged on his waistband.

"Did you hear that?" she asked, her voice a loud whisper.

"Hear what?"

"Shush!"

The two stood perfectly still, pausing in the entrance-way of Camryn's living room.

"I don't hear anything!" Darryl whispered back.

"That!" Camryn exclaimed a second time.

Darryl stood perfectly still, his head tilted just so. A distinctive hiss suddenly cut through the silence. Darryl tilted the cell phone downward and as the glint of light hit the floor, he yelled out in surprise. Before them, snakes moved smoothly, covering her hardwood floors.

"You've got to be kidding me!" Camryn exclaimed.

"Walk!" Darryl ordered, pushing her back toward the front door. "Move!"

Racing for the door, Camryn rushed back to the outside. Jumping up and down in the front yard, she cursed, profanity spilling past her lips.

Darryl dialed 911.

The police were still taking their statement when the power to Camryn's home was restored. The local utility company advised them that someone claiming to be Camryn Charles had ordered the disconnection of her own service, and the order had been fulfilled just days earlier. The duo remained in the front yard while animal control methodically gathered each serpent, dropping them into large plastic containers.

As the first containers were placed in the back of a pickup truck, Camryn moved forward to get a closer look. The animal control officer tossed her a toothless grin.

"Right many of them buggers in there!" he said.

She shook her head. "Can I take a peek?" she asked.

He nodded as he lifted the top to one of the cases, allowing her to peer inside. Reaching in, Camryn pulled out an oversize boa constrictor. She turned, holding out the snake in front of her.

Darryl shook his head at her. "You need to put that thing down, Camryn," he said as she moved toward him.

"You're squeamish!"

"I don't like snakes. In fact, I hate snakes."

As she stepped closer, Darryl took a step back. "I'm not playing with you, Camryn. Put that damn thing away."

Camryn giggled softly as she turned an about-face and returned the animal to the container. The last two snakes filled the containers, joining the others in the back of the truck.

"How many are in there?" she inquired.

The animal control guy shrugged. "We done counted 'bout two hundred of 'em so far. And that's just in the living room. 'Bout twice that many in the bedroom! We're gonna be here awhile and still no guarantee we'll get 'em all."

Camryn rolled her eyes skyward. "Unbelievable!" she exclaimed as she made her way back to Darryl's side.

"Didn't you play with bugs and snakes when you were a kid?" she said.

"We were stationed in Germany when I was a kid. They didn't have bugs and snakes."

Camryn laughed. "You big baby!" She pressed her body to his and kissed his lips.

Darryl chuckled with her. "When it comes to snakes, yes, I am," he said as he kissed her back, wrapping his arms around her waist. "The biggest baby! And I'm not ashamed to admit it, either!"

The two stood holding on to each other, watching as the cleanup continued. "Do you think you want to go back to the hotel tonight, Camryn?"

She shook her head. "No, I'm staying in my house tonight."

"Well, you'll understand if I don't stay here with you."

"What if they don't get them all?"

Darryl shrugged. "You like snakes, remember?"

"So you're not going to protect me?"

"I will gladly pay for a hotel for as long as you need, baby. And I'll stay with you to keep you company. But I'm not staying here and I prefer you didn't insist on staying either for a while."

Camryn shook her head. "I appreciate that but I'll be fine."

They were interrupted by one of the patrol officers.

"Ms. Charles?"

"Yes, sir."

"I think we've gotten all the information we'll be able to get tonight. One of the investigators from the department will call you tomorrow. We have your number to reach you, right?"

"Yes."

Darryl interjected. "I'm sure Asia Landry, my former girlfriend, is responsible for this. I gave her information to the other officer. Is anything going to be done about her?"

The officer took a quick look through his notes. "Sir, I'm sure we'll follow up, but it looks like Ms. Landry has been in California since your encounter with her at the Boudreaux work site. We just spoke to her father and he assured us that there was no way possible for his daughter to have been involved."

Darryl tossed his hands up in frustration. "Her father will say anything, but I know she did this!"

The police officer nodded politely. "Sir, I appreciate your enthusiasm and I assure you that there will be a full investigation. Until then you need to calm down."

Darryl's eyes narrowed. "I am calm," he said through gritted teeth.

Camryn drew a soothing hand down the length of his arm. "Thank you, Officer. We appreciate everything that's being done."

The man nodded, passed her his business card and headed back toward his car.

James Landry had been screaming at his daughter for two days straight. Everything he had to say to Asia seemed to go in one ear and out the other. Her latest antics had been the last straw.

"I'm sorry, Daddy!" Asia exclaimed for the umpteenth time. "It was just a silly joke."

"A silly joke, Asia? You inundated the woman's home with snakes. Snakes! That was not funny, Asia."

"They weren't poisonous," she said nonchalantly.

The man shook his head. "Why snakes?"

She shrugged, not bothering to say that Darryl feared the slithery creatures. "A joke!" she said sarcastically.

"And how much did that cost you?"

Her shoulders pushed to the ceiling a second time

as she rolled her eyes. "It won't happen again, Daddy. I promise," she said, finally lifting her eyes to his.

He shook his head again, pausing for a brief moment before continuing. "Darryl has filed a complaint about you showing up in New Orleans. You violated the court order and he's pressing charges. Our attorney says you have to appear before a judge next week. Unfortunately, daughter, there might not be any repercussions for what you did to Ms. Charles, but you will have to answer for going near that Boudreaux boy."

Asia smiled. "It's going to be okay, Daddy," she said sweetly.

The doorbell ringing interrupted the conversation.

"I'll get that," Asia chimed, jumping to her feet.

Her father dismissed her with a wave of his hand.

At the door, the delivery man gave her a warm smile. "Package for Asia Landry," he said, motioning toward the box in his hand.

Excitement shimmered in Asia's eyes. "I'm Asia Landry," she said as he passed her the brown-wrapped package. He also passed her a clipboard for her signature on the delivery receipt.

"Have a great day," he said as he turned and headed back to his delivery truck.

Asia loved surprises and presents. There was no return address on the box but she just knew it had to be from Darryl wanting to make amends. She couldn't think of anyone else who would be sending her a package and she hadn't ordered anything through the mail. She shook the box lightly, noting that something shifted inside. Her eyes widened with excitement.

Moving into the dining room, she rested the box

against the oversize table and ripped the brown paper from the package. The box had been taped and she pulled a nail across the seal to break it. Pulling at the flap and lifting the lid, Asia peered eagerly inside. She suddenly jumped back and screamed loudly as a large snake hissed and slithered up and over the side of the container.

Her father rushed into the room to see what the problem was. Spying the serpent as it slid off the table to the floor and crawled beneath the dining buffet, he shook his head from side to side, meeting his daughter's tear-filled stare. Asia stood with her back against the wall, clutching her hands to her chest. Her face was twisted in anger.

"Well, well, well," he said casually. "It looks like Ms. Charles sent you one of your pets back."

Camryn knew it was only a matter of time before Darryl discovered what she had done. She saw it on his face when he entered the office, taking a seat in the upholstered chair in front of her desk.

"You sent Asia a snake, Camryn?"

Camryn lifted her eyes from the paperwork she was reviewing. "Excuse me?"

Darryl's gaze narrowed. "You heard me."

She shrugged. "I found one in the corner of the bathroom and figured it would only be courteous to return it to her."

Darryl shook his head. A sly smile pulled at his mouth. "Please assure me that I have not gotten into bed with another crazy woman."

Camryn crossed her arms over her chest, leaning back in her seat. "Do you need to be reassured?"

"I need to know that I'm not going to wake up with a snake anywhere near me!"

"Know that I can give it as good as I get, Darryl. And I don't back down from a challenge. If you do right by me, you can trust that I will always do right by you. But on an exceptionally good day I'm the wrong one to mess with. Asia hit me on a good day. She invaded my private space. I don't take that lightly."

There was a knock on the door and Camryn's assistant peeked her head in. "Ms. Charles, is there anything else you need before I leave?"

Camryn shook her head. "No, Hazel. I appreciate you asking. I will probably be late tomorrow but I'll call you as soon as I know my schedule."

"Yes, ma'am. I'll let security know that you two are the last ones left in the building. Have a good night. Goodbye, Mr. Boudreaux."

"Good night, Hazel," Darryl responded.

The two sat staring at each other, neither saying a word. Camryn broke the silence.

"Are you upset with me?"

Darryl laughed. "Nope!"

"When did she call you?"

"She didn't. Mr. Landry called to ask if I knew anything about it."

"Was he upset?"

"Actually, it sounded like he was amused. I think he's had all he can take of Asia's antics."

Camryn took a deep breath. "I promise I will never

ever put a snake in your bed," she said, moving from behind her desk to stand in front of him.

"Or my car or anywhere else near me," Darryl intoned. "Cross your heart and pinkie swear," he said.

Staring him in the eye, Camryn unbuttoned her silk blouse. Pulling it open, she slowly made the sign of the cross just above her left breast. She reached for his hand, entwining his fingers between her own as she pulled his palm to her heart, the heel grazing her rising nipple.

"I pinkie swear," she said as she pulled her skirt up and straddled him in the chair. She wasn't wearing any panties, her bare bottom settling comfortably against him.

Darryl grinned, his head bobbing up and down. Reaching his other hand to the back of her head, he twisted his fingers in her curls and pulled her to him, kissing her passionately. Camryn eased forward until her pelvis was pressed tight against the rise of nature in his pants. Her skirt had risen up around her waist. He slid his hand from the back of her head down her back to the crest above her behind and caressed her smooth butt cheek. It was perfectly round and as slick as satin. His fingertip slid up and down the delectable valley between the cheeks, and his erection, full and engorged, twitched against the fabric of his pants, aching to be released.

Camryn continued to kiss him hungrily as she slowly ground her pelvis tight to his. As she wrapped her hands around his neck, he sensed that she desperately needed release. He reached both hands around to her butt cheeks and pulled her closer so his cock was hard against the cusp of her crotch. He eased up and then pulled her to him again and again. Camryn's body tensed and she began to pant softly, tossing her head back against her neck. Darryl continued to hump her body against his until she came against his lap, letting out a long, soft squeal. After the first spasm of her orgasm Camryn continued to thrust herself repeatedly against him, keeping her orgasm peaked. She finally thrust herself tight to him one last time, collapsing in his arms, her breathing heavy.

Darryl held her, his hands caressing her back until her breathing eased and she caught her breath. He leaned up and kissed her full on the mouth and she responded by parting her lips, allowing him to slide his tongue into the cavity. His tongue was met by hers eagerly swirling past his lips. She put her hand on the back of his neck and pulled him to her as she thrust her tongue into his open orifice.

Darryl reached up and slid his hand beneath her bra, pulling at one hardened nipple and then the other. Camryn purred, her voice raspy as she moaned his name over and over. He kneaded harder and harder, Camryn seeming to have no limits. The harder he massaged her breasts, the more excited she seemed to become.

"You like it?" he whispered huskily.

"Your hands feel so good," she moaned. "Please don't stop!"

Darryl was happy to continue, dropping his mouth to her nipples. He lashed each one with his tongue, moving back and forth eagerly. He moved his hands from her breasts back to her bottom, massaging her butt cheeks even harder. He shifted his body backward, pushing his hips and legs forward so that he was in a more reclined position. He continued to knead her buttocks with one hand as he licked her neck and chest with wild abandon.

He slipped two of his fingers into Camryn's mouth and she sucked greedily, wetting them with her saliva. The sensation was intense, the pulsing sensation coursing through every fiber of his body.

Pulling his hand from her mouth Darryl slid his wet fingers up across her perineum, gently massaging the soft skin from the back edge of her vagina up between each of her butt cheeks. Camryn let out a loud moan as he continued to massage her, working his way till his fingertip found her tight ring. She pressed her butt against his hand and Darryl took the cue, pressing his finger into her. Her hole was tight but also giving as he entered her smoothly, stopping at the second knuckle. It wrapped snuggly around his finger, offering little strong resistance. Camryn moaned again, pressing her face into his neck, licking at the spot beneath his chin. She didn't resist or flinch when he penetrated her anally, allowing a second and then a third finger into her posterior cavity. The mere thought made Darryl's member pulse with a vengeance.

Camryn continued to suck and lick his neck and ears, leaving a large welt to remind him of their lovemaking for a few days after. She licked down to his nipples and sucked one until it was tender, flicking her tongue over the hardened nub. They were both in a high state of arousal as Darryl thrust his pelvis up and down, desperately needing to orgasm.

Rising from his seat, Darryl lifted her with him, wrapping her legs around his waist. He held her by the

waist with one hand as he slipped the other between
them, releasing himself from his pants. His slacks fell
to the floor beneath his feet and he stepped out of them.
Darryl moved her against the wall, her back pressed
against the ivory paint. His hands clutched her buttocks, holding her up as he pressed himself between
her legs. Camryn reached down to grab his manhood,
stroking him boldly.

Darryl could feel an orgasm beginning to churn
through his pelvis up into his abdomen. Camryn sensed
it, too, as she guided him toward her entrance, pushing
her pelvis up and onto him. Darryl entered her secret
box easily, pushing and pulling himself in and out of
her. He pushed her harder against the drywall, hump-
ing her body vigorously. Camryn's arms were latched
tightly around his neck, her legs locked together around
his lower back as she rocked back and forth with him.
Her mouth clung to his and there was no defining where
her body ended and his began. They were one unit,
moving in perfect sync, and then she spasmed, the satin
lining of her inner walls pulsing around his manhood,
the sensation moving him to climax with her.

As they sank to the carpeted floor, both were panting heavily. Both their bodies were shooting mini af-
tershocks through their relaxing muscles. As they lay
together, Camryn resting on top of Darryl's chest, she
reached down to wrap her warm hand around his manhood. Her touch was light and easy, the tips of her fingers feeling like feathers teasing his skin. Darryl was
suddenly surprised when he twitched, his temperature
rising as she revived life back into the appendage. He

saw her smile, clearly pleased with the results of her ministrations.

"Girl, what are you doing to me?" he whispered huskily.

Camryn giggled softly. "It's more so what you are going to do to me," she responded as she continued to reawaken vivacity in his member.

He grinned. "And what am I going to be doing?"

Smiling back, Camryn slid her body from his, pulling at the clothes that were still tangled around her body. Darryl sat up, sliding his back against the wall to watch her. Moving onto her hands and knees, she slowly gyrated her buttocks from side to side. He skimmed his hand over his crotch, slightly amazed at just how hard he was, the blood surging through his veins with a vengeance. And then she leaned forward, resting her chest against the floor as she spread her butt cheeks apart with her hands.

Tossing him a quick look over her shoulder, Camryn beckoned him forward with her eyes. "Be gentle," she cooed.

His eyes wide, Darryl crawled up behind her, placing both of his hands against the line of her hips. He palmed the fullness of each melon, leaning to bite the soft skin. Darryl suddenly knew that it wouldn't take much for him to explode with pleasure. He took three deep breaths to stall the wave of heat threatening to consume him.

"Do me," Camryn intoned, her raspy voice like fuel on the fire.

Darryl eased himself against her rectum and she tensed ever so slightly, her body quivering with anticipation. He slowly trailed his fingers against her opening until he felt her relax. As his other hand slipped around her waist to tease her clit, he slid himself over her.

"Give it to me," she urged.

Slowly and easily, Darryl eased himself through her rear door. He bit down against his bottom lip as Camryn pushed her muscles to allow him entrance. His fingers continued to dance against her swollen nub as he sank himself deeper and deeper inside of her.

Camryn suddenly moved her body from his, pulling forward until only the tip of his manhood was inside of her. She rested only briefly before she pushed back until he was buried as far as his tool could go. She repeated the motion twice, then paused again as Darryl throbbed, every muscle in his body heated. When he couldn't take it anymore, he took control, plunging and retreating with reckless abandon, the most decadent sensations sweeping between them. Pumping back and forth, Darryl's own buttocks flexed with every forward push and backward pull. Back and forth, until he tensed, shuddered, groaned and pushed hard into Camryn's bottom.

"Oh!" Camryn moaned in ecstasy and then she cried out with pleasure first, her muscles like a vise gripping him hard. Darryl trembled excitedly as he exploded with a huge sigh and then he slumped and collapsed on top of her spent body.

With his arms wrapped around her, Darryl held her tightly to him. Camryn wiggled sweetly against him, her bottom still pressed tight against his crotch. She purred ever so softly.

"You okay?" Darryl asked, his voice barely a whisper.

She purred louder. "Better than okay."

Darryl pressed a kiss against the curve of her shoulder. "Baby, you are just full of surprises."

Chapter 14

Asia was under house arrest for violating her probation. If her father had not been willing to assume full responsibility for her, she would have found herself residing in the county jail for six months. She sighed as she lifted her left leg to eye the government-issued bracelet that decorated her ankle. Her father found the whole situation humorous but Asia was not amused.

She blew another deep sigh as she surfed the internet, catching up on the news in New Orleans. Nola.com had headlined the governor's position on taxes, the murder of a young college student, the high score mounted by the LSU basketball team, and a photo gallery of zebras and ostriches racing at the Fair Grounds.

Asia clinked link after link, briefly scanning each article. It had become a bad habit, her daily search for any news about Darryl and Camryn. Just days ago there had been news of Boudreaux Towers and both had been mentioned for their involvement in the project. She clicked the local Living tab and scanned the page. As she prepared to shut down her computer, one link suddenly caught her attention: LOCAL ROYALTY CELEBRATE ENGAGEMENT.

Clicking the pale blue icon, she held her breath as the page loaded. The headline spilled across the screen beside a photograph of Darryl and Camryn posed arm in arm. They were staring deep into each other's eyes, smiling sweetly. Camryn's left hand rested gently against Darryl's chest and there was no missing the large diamond that adorned her ring finger.

Perusing the article, Asia learned that the two families had formally announced the couple's engagement. Darryl had asked Camryn to marry him. They were planning a holiday wedding and the who's who of New Orleans had celebrated the news at a gala party held in the Crescent City Ballroom of the Roosevelt Hotel.

Asia finally let go of the breath she'd been holding. Tears misted her eyes, pooling behind her eyelids. She took another glance at her ankle bracelet as she contemplated her options. With a mountain of ideas spinning through her head, she knew there was no way she could do anything to stop the nuptials without a little help from a friend. Shutting down the computer, Asia called out to the only friend she had. "Daddy! Daddy! Where are you?"

Darryl slept soundly beside her, sprawled on his back, a hand tossed over his eyes. Camryn had been tossing and turning for hours, unable to rest. There was too much happening too quickly and she was beginning to feel the pressure.

Construction on Boudreaux Towers was moving along nicely. She loved to stand across the street from the work site watching as the building took form, beginning to tower above the landscape. Everything about her design was taking shape nicely. Most of Darryl's time was spent on-site, dealing with the contractor, the workmen and the inspectors. Their weekly meetings with Mason and her father had both men confident that Darryl and Camryn were getting the job done. So much so that Mason had disappeared overseas with his wife for a vacation and Kenneth Charles and his son, Carson, had taken a few weeks to enjoy a deep-sea-fishing excursion.

Planning a wedding was well out of Camryn's comfort zone. She would never have fathomed there being so much that needed to be done. She was beginning to think that a trip downtown to the justice of the peace was a better idea. But each time she got together with the women in Darryl's family, their exuberance incited her own. She was grateful for his sister Maitlyn, who'd returned from her trip rested and happy and excited to assume the responsibilities of being their wedding planner. The woman called her daily to question her wants and Darryl's wishes but even with her helping hand Camryn was overwhelmed.

She also found herself challenged with another venture, an invitation having come to submit a proposal for an international project. Camryn was excited to find herself on the short list for a multibillion-dollar construction assignment in the sovereign state of Dubai, in the Middle East. If awarded the job, Camryn would work directly for the ruling sheikh and his family, affording her the opportunity to cement her name in architectural history. Reading through the prospectus had kindled her creative spirit—so much so that she had immediately begun to do her research, taking time away from all the other things on her to-do list. And with her and Darryl's rigid schedules, she still hadn't had a chance to discuss the opportunity with him.

She rolled over on her side and, unable to get comfortable, rolled over onto the other. Darryl suddenly opened his eyes, lifting his gaze to stare at her.

"What's wrong, baby?"

She shook her head against the mattress as she curled her body against his. "I can't sleep," she whispered. "I didn't mean to wake you."

Darryl shrugged. "You want me to get you something? Warm milk, wine, a glass of water?"

"No, darling, just go back to sleep."

Darryl eased an arm beneath her and pulled her against him. She was naked and the warmth of her bare skin felt good against his own.

"You feel good," he hummed as he caressed her easily.

"So do you," Camryn said, cuddling into the curve of his arm. She trailed her fingers across his chest and abdomen. She was suddenly hungry for him, reaching between his legs to take hold of his maleness. She smiled when his organ twitched in her hand.

"Mmm! Now just look at what you've done!" Darryl murmured.

Camryn rolled above him, lifting her body up to

straddle his. She squatted over him with her feet planted flat on either side of his hips. She lowered herself down as she held his penis in her hand, placing the tip of it at the entrance to her most private place. In one swift motion she lowered herself down on his member until he was completely buried inside of her. Putting both of her hands on Darryl's chest, she lowered her knees, holding him tightly inside of herself as she worked her inner muscles, milking him easily.

The sweet sensation of her velvet lining wrapped around his engorged member was intense and Darryl let out a long deep groan. With narrowed eyes he watched her as she sat impaled on his organ, her head thrown back in ecstasy. Her own eyes were half closed, her mouth open as she moaned softly.

"You fill me up so nicely," Camryn purred. "This feels so hot!"

"That's it, baby," Darryl extolled as she rode him, thrusting herself against him. He groaned with her.

She began to raise and lower herself on his glistening member. He had never been so hard or engorged, the veins along his shaft pulsing with his heartbeat. She was completely mesmerizing as she slid up the length of him until the head of his manhood just kissed her entrance and then slammed her body hard against him, thrusting him deeper inside of her.

He was just thrusts away from coming. Reaching around her torso, he pulled her toward him, wrapping an arm around her waist. Darryl flipped her onto her back and climbed between her legs. He grabbed her behind the knees and pushed her limbs forward, raising her hips to make his penetration easier. Camryn gasped loudly as he lined himself against her and pushed forward, reentering her slick hole with one deep thrust. Gripping her buttocks, he lifted her easily, thrusting himself in and out of her, Camryn meeting him stroke for stroke. She reached her orgasm then and her taut muscles gripped him tightly, forcing him to fire like a cannon deep inside of her.

Falling against him, Camryn savored the sweetness of each tremor, every muscle in her body feeling like melting jelly. Nestling herself against his chest, she closed her eyes and fell into a deep sleep, Darryl's arms wrapped tightly around her.

"So what have you decided, Camryn?" Kenneth questioned, his eyes meeting his daughter's stare.

The two were sitting with Darryl and Mason over breakfast, reviewing an issue with the electrical construction for Boudreaux Towers. With the details settled, Kenneth was ready to move on to the next item on his agenda.

"I'm sorry, Father," she responded, a confused expression crossing her face. "What have I decided about what?"

The man stared at her with a raised brow. "About Dubai. Have you made a decision?"

Darryl turned to stare at her as Camryn cut her eye in his direction. "Dubai? What about Dubai?"

"You haven't told Darryl yet?" Kenneth admonished. "Are you even considering it, Camryn?" He leaned forward in his seat, staring at his daughter intently.

Camryn rolled her eyes as she reached for her chicory coffee and took a swig. "No, Father, I haven't had a chance to tell Darryl." She paused and took·another swig of her drink. "Darryl, I need to talk to you about an opportunity that's recently come up in Dubai. Before my father's announcement I was hoping that we would discuss it at lunch today." She glanced nervously at Darryl.

His expression was stunned. "Please tell me you're not talking about the new Shorouk Al Shams Compound." Darryl said.

Camryn eyed him with surprise. "You've heard about it?"

"Anybody in the industry worth their salt has heard about it. The architect that wins that job will be renowned around the world."

Kenneth nodded. "Camryn received an invitation from Sheikh Muhammad himself to submit a proposal and design. They want her to fly to Dubai next week to survey the site and meet the royal family. From what I've learned, she's one of three architects they're considering. I know one of them is the team that did the world's tallest hotel."

Darryl jumped up excitedly. He grabbed Camryn around the shoulders, lifting her from the chair and spinning her around. "Baby, that's wonderful!"

"Congratulations!" Mason chimed in.

Camryn held up her hands as Darryl set her back on her feet. "Hold on for a minute. Yes, it is exciting, but with everything going on I don't think it's a viable option right now."

"Camryn, you cannot pass up this opportunity," Darryl exclaimed. "The top architectural firms in the world have created designs in Dubai. The Burj Al Arab, that tallest hotel, is just the beginning!"

"I've spent time there," Mason said casually, "and it is something. It's the epitome of luxury and opulence. One of my most memorable hotel stays."

Darryl nodded. "Let's not forget the man-made islands just offshore! And isn't Dubai where they have that underwater hotel?"

"Yes," Camryn responded, "it's the Water Discus Hotel. It's surrounded by a coral reef with twenty-one rooms that are like ten meters below the surface and look out on the ocean floor. And that is *exactly* why I'm still thinking about it! This is a *huge* project! And whatever I come up with is going to have to outshine every other building in Dubai."

She took a deep breath and held it before continuing. "I still have responsibilities to Boudreaux Towers. Then there's the wedding, Darryl. We also have house shopping, not to mention moving. It's just too much, honey!"

Darryl grabbed her hands, kissing her palms and fingers. "If you pass this up, please make sure it's only because you don't want to do it. If you want this, Camryn, we can figure out a way to make it work."

She stared into his eyes. The look he was giving her was promising, and it said that there was nothing the two of them couldn't accomplish if they put their minds to it. As she glanced from her father to Mason and back, both men seemed to be giving their support, as well.

She took another deep breath.

"Do you want this, Camryn?" Darryl asked.

"I don't know. I… Well…it's…" she stammered.

Darryl persisted. "It's a yes-or-no answer, Camryn. Yes or no. Do you want this amazing opportunity?"

She paused as she met his gaze and held it, her head bobbing up and down against her shoulders. "Yes!"

Darryl grinned widely. He tossed Mason a quick look. "Big brother, do you think we can borrow your plane next week? Camryn's going to Dubai!"

Chapter 15

Darryl was resting on Camryn's living room sofa, his legs stretched out across the furniture. Unwinding, he sat with the latest Walter Mosley novel in his lap and a frosted bottle of Guinness stout on the end table at his elbow. Standing in the doorway of her living room, she couldn't begin to fathom how she'd gotten so lucky. Darryl made her laugh and she always felt comfortable in his presence. The man loved and supported her and she had absolutely no doubts of his affection.

Camryn had to admit that she was excited about the future he'd fantasized for them: partnered in business, in marriage and in life. Darryl wanted children and until he'd shared his dreams of raising two little mini-Darryls and a teeny-weeny Camryn, she hadn't given any consideration to babies in her life. Now she was excited at the prospect of carrying his child and raising his children, although she'd joked that she would only settle for two teeny-weeny Camryns and one mini-Darryl.

They'd already committed to their first home together, a six-thousand-square-foot bungalow on Jefferson Avenue. The home inspection had been a win-win for the sellers and for them, and they were on schedule to close escrow in two weeks. Darryl planned to move in first. They'd decided that Camryn would not move in until after the wedding. But there was still the negotiation of space, the acquisition of new furniture and the blending of their personal items that needed to be accomplished.

Boudreaux Towers was in its final stages. The exterior of the building was done and finished, the contractor and his crew focused on the building's interior. They no longer had to contend with inclement weather, so the construction schedule was tight. Darryl spent more time on-site than he did in his office. Both their days started early and most nights by the time they reached home, it was past time for bed.

They planned to exchange vows on New Year's Eve. Both she and Darryl loved the idea of starting their lives as a married couple during the holidays, when their family and friends were celebrating together. Despite her father and Darryl's parents wanting them to have a large wedding, they had decided on an intimate gathering of immediate family only followed by a large reception that would include family, friends and close business associates. It was the holiday event everyone wanted to get an invitation to and planning that spectacular celebration came with its own challenges. Camryn was grateful for Darryl's sister. The woman was a lifesaver as far as she was concerned.

So considering that the two of them were already pressed for personal time to get things done, she was still at odds about how she was going to balance an international project in the mix. Especially, if she was being honest, an international project that she really wanted. If she were to win the bid to design the multibillion-dollar retail and housing complex in Dubai, it would be the pinnacle of her career. The fact that she was actually being considered simply blew her away.

Camryn believed Darryl when he said that they could figure it out. She trusted that if anyone could help her make it happen, Darryl could. Standing in the doorway, her arms wrapped around her torso, Camryn felt herself smiling warmly, completely enamored as she stood watching him.

Strolling into the room, Camryn moved in behind him, wrapping her arms around his shoulders. She hugged him tightly and pressed a damp kiss to the side of his neck.

"Hey," Darryl said. He tilted his head to kiss her lips. "Is everything okay?"

Camryn nodded. "I wanted to apologize to you."

"For what, baby?" Darryl said. He pulled her around the side of the sofa, holding her hand as he guided her to sit in his lap. "What did you do?"

She met his gaze and smiled. Wrapping her arms around his waist, she hugged him again as she leaned her head against his broad chest. "I'm sorry that you had to hear about the Dubai invitation from my father before you heard it from me."

Darryl nodded slowly. "I'm glad you brought that up. I was going to ask you why you kept that from me."

She shrugged. "I really wasn't trying to hide it from you. I've just been so overwhelmed with it all."

"We have a lot going on. Do you want to postpone the wedding?" Darryl queried.

She shook her head vehemently. "No, I don't! I can't believe you'd ask me that."

"Baby, I'm not saying that we shouldn't get married at all. I'm saying that we could just delay the wedding and get married in the spring. Or get married after you've finished designing the Dubai building. We have options."

"No, we don't. We have a wedding planned for December 31 and that's when we're getting married. Don't think you're going to leave me at the altar, Darryl Boudreaux!"

Darryl laughed. "Yes, ma'am!" he said as he leaned to kiss her lips. "I can't wait to marry you, Ms. Charles!"

Darryl shifted his body so that she could recline easily with him. "So, tell me more about the project."

"You really know as much as I know. The building has been commissioned by the reigning sheikh. Whoever is selected will report directly to the royal family. I'm thinking that if I win the bid, I'll have to stay in Dubai for a short period of time, but probably no more than two, maybe three months in the beginning. Boudreaux Towers should be completed by the time we get to that stage and you'll be able to come to Dubai with me. You'd want to come with me, wouldn't you?"

"Of course!"

"Because I wouldn't want us to be away from each

other for that long, Darryl. I couldn't do it if I thought it would mean we'd be separated."

He kissed her again. "Well, let's go to Dubai. We'll see what they're proposing. You submit your bid and design and we'll make our decision after they award you the contract."

"What if I don't win?" Camryn said, her eyes widening. "I mean, I might not get the job."

Darryl smiled. "Do you really believe that?"

"Anything is possible, Darryl," Camryn answered.

He shook his head, lifting his book back into his lap as he went back to his reading.

"Is that how you do me?" she said teasingly.

Darryl chuckled. "You have work to do. So go design the building of the century."

"I am not going back to the office tonight," Camryn noted. "Not tonight."

Darryl nodded his agreement. "You don't have to. Why don't you go look in your spare bedroom."

"My spare bedroom?" Camryn said curiously. "What's going on in my spare bedroom?"

Darryl shrugged. "I guess you have to go look," he said, a curious expression on his face.

Camryn gave him a look as she jumped to her feet. Darryl followed behind her as she headed down the hall to her rear bedroom. Since moving into the home, Camryn hadn't bothered to do anything with the room. It had become storage space, catching everything Camryn had needed to tuck away from public view.

The door to the room was closed. With her excitement rising, she paused, her hand on the doorknob. She tossed Darryl a glance over her shoulder before turning the latch and pushing the door open. Her smile widened tenfold.

Darryl had moved all her clutter from the space. He'd replicated her office space, decorating the room with a large conference table, a drafting table, a comfortable sofa and images of her favorite artwork. She turned to meet his gaze as he stood in the doorway watching her take it all in.

"Of course," Darryl stated, "we'll set up office for you in the new house but I figured if you're able to work from home more easily, then that might help take some of the pressure off of you."

Camryn threw herself into his arms and kissed him, her lips dancing sweetly over his. "Darryl Boudreaux, I think I love you!"

He grinned broadly. "Camryn Charles, I know you love me," he responded.

She grinned with him. "Yeah, I think you're right. In fact, sir, I'm pretty sure that I am truly all yours!"

The Boudreaux jet was waiting for them on the tarmac. Within minutes of their boarding, the pilot cleared them for takeoff.

"Wow!" Camryn exclaimed. "Your brother has a really sweet thing going on here!" she said as she peered out the airplane's window.

Darryl laughed. "Mason's definitely living large," he said.

Camryn settled back in the leather seat. "Very large!"

"My brother has worked exceptionally hard for all his success. I'm really proud of the old guy."

"All of your family is quite impressive."

"They're your family now, too, Camryn. Everyone really loves you."

Camryn smiled brightly, having no need to say a word.

The estimated travel time from New Orleans to Dubai was some twenty-plus hours. They were scheduled to stop in Spain and then Turkey before landing in the United Arab Emirates. Camryn was excited about the venture, although the possibility of what it might mean for her future, and for Darryl's, was slightly unnerving. Darryl's exuberance was fuel enough for them both.

They talked for the first few hours, confirming wedding details, hypothesizing about the outcome of the election and sharing tales from their youth. Camryn had drifted off to sleep first, nothing but snow-white clouds cushioning their travels and her dreams. Darryl had dozed off with her, delighted to see her finally rest. She'd been working nonstop for the last few days trying to put everything into place. He was exceptionally proud of her, knowing that her talent knew no bounds. He also knew that she was nervous and he was doing everything in his power to calm any anxiety she might have been experiencing.

Midtrip, Camryn had pulled him into the plane's restroom, claiming that she had a problem that only he could handle. Minutes later she inducted him into the Mile-High Club, the two of them making love to each other in the stall. Falling asleep a second time, neither woke until the flight attendant announced their landing in Barcelona, Spain.

They lunched at the Café de L'Academia, the de-

lightful restaurant highly recommended by Mason and
Camryn's father. Under different circumstances it might
have been difficult to find, but thanks to Mason and
Maitlyn, a car was waiting to escort them to their destination.

Darryl ordered for them both and Camryn thoroughly enjoyed the duck pâté and truffle toasted sand-
wich. They had the Spanish version of crème brûlée for
dessert. The meal was wonderfully leisurely and sitting
outside beneath the warm sunshine boosted her spirit.
When they left, there was a fiesta in the little square
and they took a brief moment to join in with the dancing. By the time they returned to the airport, the jet had
been refueled, both the pilot and copilot were rested,
and they were ready to take off. Some six hours later
they were enjoying dinner in Istanbul. Mason and his
staff had arranged for them to spend the night so that
they would be well rested when they arrived the next
morning in Dubai.

A representative of the royal family was there to
meet them at the airport. His name was Sami and he
was a charming personality dressed in the traditional
long-sleeved white robes and headscarf, or *kaffiyeh,* of
his Bedouin ancestors. His English was near perfect
and he chattered on nonstop as he helped them navi-
gate through the Dubai airport and maneuver their way
through customs.

Camryn was in awe of the facility, a contemporary
mass of stainless steel and glass. Before escorting them
to their hotel, Sami gave them a tour of the city, chauf-
feuring them in a polished silver-gray Bentley. Dubai
was a jaw-dropping oasis of stone and glass and mar-

ble and concrete. Twice the size of London, England, it was a dazzling display of wealth and riches. Camryn couldn't begin to imagine how she was going to compete.

"It's fantastical," she said, meeting Darryl's gaze as they pulled up to the infamous Burj Al Arab. A testament to human ingenuity, the hotel was Dubai's equivalent of the Eiffel Tower, towering over every other building in the world. The couple exchanged glances when Sami told them the hotel's rooms rented for a minimum of $17,000 per night and that the sheikh had arranged for them to stay in one of their luxury suites, the accommodations coming with a private manservant and white Rolls-Royce for their exclusive use.

As Sami checked them into their room, Darryl couldn't help but whisper that Camryn's design for the new compound had to ensure the country's, and its ruler's, position on the global map. The level of sheer decadence required to maintain the standards of the land would be a tall order for any architect to meet.

Camryn nodded her agreement. "I know. I realize the crazier the idea, the better," she said. "It has to be over-the-top!"

Darryl could see her mind spinning and he ran a warm hand across her back, patting her gently with pride. When they were checked into the hotel and settled in their room, Sami filled them in on their schedule.

"The sheikh and his wife will be hosting a reception for you at four o'clock, followed by dinner at six. Tomorrow you'll meet with the project team in the morning to discuss what the family is wanting. And in the afternoon, we have a real estate agent who has been assigned to show you available properties for your stay, should you be awarded the contract. Then we hope that you'll take advantage of our beautiful city on Thursday at your leisure."

"Which wife?" Darryl inquired.

Camryn tossed him a wide-eyed look as Sami answered.

"His senior wife, Princess Maryam. She tends to keep more of a low profile than his junior wife, Princess Latifa, but this project is very dear to her. The compound will be built on the land her father included in her dowry. His junior wife will join you for dinner."

Nodding her appreciation, Camryn promised to be ready when Sami returned to escort them to the sheikh's private home. Behind closed doors, she and Darryl discussed the absurdity of their surroundings, everything larger, decadent and more abundant than anything they had ever experienced.

"Mason warned me, but this is more than I could have ever anticipated," Darryl said.

"It's extravagant to the nth degree," Camryn added. She glanced down to the watch on her wrist. "Why don't we get a shower and a quick nap before we have to be ready."

Darryl laughed. "You know you're breaking the law," he teased.

"What?"

"We're not legally married, so we can't be making love and shouldn't be spending the night together. It's against the law here."

"We haven't made love in Dubai yet. So I haven't broken the law if I haven't done anything."

Darryl eased his body against hers. "Oh, you're about to do something. As soon as you get out of those clothes and get in that shower, you're going to be doing something."

Camryn kissed him, cupping his rising erection in the palm of her hand.

"Yep!" Darryl gasped. "You are about to break some serious laws!"

Camryn laughed. "Mmm. Well, if you don't tell, I won't tell," she said as she led the way to the oversize bathroom, dropping articles of her clothing like a trail of bread crumbs.

"I'm not telling anyone anything!" Darryl said as he followed behind her, leaving his own trail of clothing from the living room to the marbled bathroom.

The immense space was easily in a league of its own. Camryn imagined they could have fit a whole football team inside the large glass shower. As she stepped into the enclosure and turned on the spray of warm water, she marveled at the stone tiles that decorated the space.

Lifting her face to the warm stream, she savored the sensation of water raining over her torso and down to her manicured toes. Darryl stepped in behind her, pressing his body easily against her, and the sensation of his hardness and body heat triggered a rush of tremors to ripple through her feminine spirit. She smiled and purred as she relaxed into the moment.

Reaching for a bar of lavender-scented goat's milk soap, Darryl lathered his hands, then trailed the suds over her shoulders and down the length of her arms. He soaped her back and buttocks, then reached around to lather her breasts and abdomen. When he slipped his fingers between her legs, Camryn parted them to make his exploration easier. Her legs were suddenly like rubber, every muscle quivering with pleasure as Darryl stroked and teased her gently. His fingertips moved lightly across the rising nub of her clitoris, tenderly parting the folds of her labia. She was trembling so much from the sheer pleasure of his touch that she had to press her palms against the shower wall to brace herself. Darryl's hands felt incredible.

He entered her from behind, suds lubricating his journey. Camryn felt herself open to him easily, his elongated member eagerly finding its way back home. Darryl pushed against the back of her neck as he pulled her hips back against his pelvis. The shift in position allowed him to plow deeper into her, slamming himself in and out of her body, his body slapping at her buttocks. The sensations were overwhelming, currents of energy pulsing through both of them.

Camryn gasped as Darryl suddenly gripped her by the neck with one hand, pulling her back to his chest. His other hand was wrapped around her waist, his fingertips dancing just at the edge of her clit. She moaned loudly, calling his name over and over again, the prayerful mantra encouraging his ministrations. He stroked her, his cock swelling fuller and fuller as he felt his climax rising.

Darryl suddenly felt as if his manhood was on fire as Camryn's body pulsed heatedly around him. Her muscles gripped him hard, milking every ounce of energy out of his body. It became more than he could handle and he screamed as he slid into her one last time. The intensity of their orgasm had the room spinning in circles. Darryl clutched the shower bar, fighting not to collapse heavily against her. Her own body was spent as she shivered, her chest pressed tight to the shower wall. Together, they slowly slid to the shower floor, the water above still warm as it sprayed them down.

"Damn!" Darryl exclaimed. "That was incredible," he muttered softly as he rolled onto his behind, his legs stretched out.

Camryn leaned her body against his, her own legs bent at the knees and spread open. She purred in agreement, a low hum rising out of her throat. "If we're going to be arrested," she teased, "it was definitely worth the risk."

Chapter 16

Darryl wore a black silk suit, white shirt, and black-and-grey-striped tie. Being respectful of the culture, Camryn's attire was stylish but conservative. She wore a simple black-and-white Carolina Herrera dress. The ankle-length black skirt was full and pleated. The blouse top was white and tailored, buttoned to the neck with long sleeves that were cuffed at her wrists. There was nothing conservative about the four-inch red-bottomed pumps that she wore. Darryl nodded his approval.

"You look stunning," he said. He leaned to press a kiss to her temple.

"Thank you. You look quite dashing yourself."

When the phone rang announcing Sami's arrival, Camryn took a deep breath, fighting to stall the ripples bubbling in the pit of her stomach.

Darryl took her hand, kissing the back of her fingers. "I am very proud of you," he said softly. "Knock 'em dead, baby! You can do this!"

Hours later Camryn lay wide awake reflecting on the night's events. Before he'd dozed off, she and Darryl had talked through each and every detail. Darryl's assessments had been important to her and she appreciated the advice he offered on how she should proceed.

Meeting the constitutional monarch of Dubai was not without its challenges. Camryn had been concerned about being respectful of his Muslim culture while being true to her own confident spirit. Women in positions of authority were still somewhat of an anomaly in the Middle Eastern culture, the female sex being expected to be seen and not always heard. Camryn had been afraid of being too direct and viewed as aggressive or disrespectful. She was mindful of not doing anything that would be construed as insulting. More than once Darryl had to tell her to relax, reminding her to simply be herself.

Sheikh Muhammad was a dashing leader, personable and completely intrigued by the excesses of Western culture. He honored his two wives and officially acknowledged some twenty-three children—nine sons and fourteen daughters. He was also quite the poet and an avid sports enthusiast. He was enthralled to learn that Darryl had actually once played a pickup game of basketball with Charles Barkley and Michael Jordan. Camryn had found that sliver of information intriguing, as well.

The two had connected nicely when the sheikh had discovered Camryn's passion for thoroughbred horses.

He was a major figure in thoroughbred horse racing and breeding. His owning numerous horse farms around the world, one in Versailles, Kentucky, made for engaging conversation, allowing Camryn to showcase her knowledge about more than architectural styles. The sheikh's discovery that she and her father owned three colts of their own broke the ice and by the end of the evening she was feeling quite comfortable about the possibility of working for the man.

When the sheikh, Darryl and the other men had disappeared into the sheikh's private library, Camryn had enjoyed her conversations with both Mrs. Muhammads.

The senior Mrs. Muhammad preferred to stay out of the public eye, following the traditions and cultures of the region. She rarely interacted with other men and because of her affinity for the project, she strongly indicated her desire to see a woman win the bid, allowing her greater opportunity for offering her opinions and being involved. The junior Mrs. Muhammad had been educated abroad, studying at Oxford University and Harvard. She was definitely more of a free spirit and she and Camryn connected instantly. The two women were instrumental in making Camryn comfortable and she found it intriguing to discover more about their two marital relationships.

Camryn knew that polygamy existed all over the world as an aspect of certain cultures or religions. Seeing it practiced up close and personal was an eye-opener. According to the Muslim Koran, a man could have up to four wives. The husband is required to treat all of his wives equally. In Sheikh Muhammad's case, each of his wives had their own home and the man's wealth ensured both lived exceptionally well.

The senior wife had explained that marriage was considered a binding contract between a man and a woman, the responsibilities of each clearly outlined. Her parents had negotiated her contract when she was a little girl, and the union had been consummated when she'd turned twenty-one. The junior wife had married him after a very intense courtship. Both women had brought very substantial dowries to the table and both seemed extremely content with the arrangement the three of them shared.

As Darryl shifted, rolling over onto his side, Camryn took a deep breath and blew a deep gust of air past her lips. He smiled ever so slightly in his sleep, an easy bend to his mouth that appeared and then disappeared just as quickly. Camryn was thankful for what she had with Darryl. She couldn't begin to imagine a life where she had to share her man with anyone. She trusted that Darryl would forever be faithful to her and only her. Fidelity would never be an issue between them.

After meeting the royal family, she and Darryl had joked about it, Darryl saying that he figured another two wives would work out nicely for them. He'd teased that he would always let her be the senior wife. Camryn had teased back about wives two and three not having much of him to work with once she was done with him.

Camryn giggled ever so slightly, the soft lilt of her laugh breaking through the silence in the room. Darryl's eyes opened and he reached out an arm in her direction. Smiling, she shifted down in the bed, easing her naked body against his. Darryl curled his own nakedness around her, the heat between them like a comfortable blanket wrapped around them. He kissed her shoulder, then nuzzled his face in the locks of her hair. He hummed softly in her ear as he drifted back off into a restful sleep.

An hour later Camryn sat in front of her computer giving substance to the best idea she'd had in a very long time. Taking advantage of the time difference between Dubai and the United States, Camryn had placed two telephone calls seeking assistance. Her father had been excited for her. Mason had been instrumental in helping her accomplish the task that was paramount on her mind. She couldn't wait for the opportunity to share the details with Darryl.

Camryn had been a nervous wreck for a total of ten minutes before Sami came to escort her to the sheikh's business offices. For ten minutes she battled an anxiety attack that had her stomach churning, perspiration beading in the palms of her hands and tears misting her eyes. And then Darryl had asked her if she was finished.

"What?" Camryn demanded, coming to a halt mid-pace.

"I asked if you were done yet."

"What do you mean?"

"I *mean* are you done and finished yet? Because you need to be finished before the car gets here for you. You need to be on top of your game, and right now you doubt yourself, and doubting yourself has you panicking. We didn't fly halfway around the world for you to crash and burn while panicking, so you really need to wrap things up and be done," he said matter-of-factly. He stood with his hands on his hips, his eyebrows raised. The silly expression on his face made her laugh.

"Point taken," she said, her head waving from side to side. She shook her hands and arms out at her sides, running in place quickly. After taking two deep breaths, the nerves slowly subsided.

Darryl nodded just as a knock registered at the door. "That would probably be Sami," he said.

"I can't do this by myself," she said suddenly.

Darryl was taken aback by her comment. "Camryn, this will be a breeze for you."

She shook her head vehemently. "That's not what I meant. Yes, I can do this by myself, but no, I don't want to."

His gaze narrowed ever so slightly.

"I need you to come with me," she said. She glanced at her watch. "How long will it take you to jump into a suit?"

"Baby, I'm not understanding—" Darryl started.

"I'll explain in the car," she interrupted. "Just please go get ready."

There was another knock on the door, Sami growing more persistent.

"I got this," Camryn responded as she moved toward the entrance. "You need to get a move on it, please!" She swung the entrance open as Darryl turned back toward the bedroom, disappearing behind the closed door.

Sami greeted her warmly and she politely asked him to carry her briefcase down to the car, assuring him that she and Darryl would both be on their way promptly.

Sami nodded. "He does not like to be kept waiting," the man said.

Camryn nodded back. "I assure you," she said, "we would never keep the sheikh waiting."

Minutes later Darryl reentered. He'd selected the charcoal-gray silk suit with a pale blue dress shirt and red-and-gray necktie. He looked like the consummate professional that he was.

"So are you going to tell me what's going on?" Darryl asked as Camryn moved back across the room to kiss his cheek. "Because you don't need me to do this with you, Camryn. I was planning on playing golf while you were gone."

"I'll explain it all in the car," she said. "I just need you to trust me."

Darryl smiled. "You are so cute when you're about to impress a roomful of people," he said.

She grinned, her brilliant white smile shimmering in the morning light. "I am cute," she said as she spun back toward the door, gesturing for him to follow.

Darryl watched her exit, admiring her rear view. Her hips swayed from side to side, the sexy shimmy of her buttocks causing heat to quiver through his groin. "Too damn cute," he muttered under his breath as he fell into step behind her.

Down in the luxury limo Darryl questioned her for the second time. She could tell by the expression on his face that he wanted a serious answer. She took a deep breath and then explained.

"I was under the impression that we would need to be here for the first few months of the project. I'm now told they would actually want us to be here for the entirety of the project. We'd be looking at three, maybe four years here in Dubai."

Darryl cut an eye at her. "Four years?"

She nodded. "How do you feel about that?"

He took a deep breath, his brow furrowing in thought as he answered. "It's definitely something we'll have to discuss. But I'll be honest, Camryn—I hadn't considered putting my own career on hold for that long."

"You wouldn't have to," she said, her bright eyes meeting his.

"What do you mean?"

Camryn took another deep breath. She reached down to the floor for her briefcase and pulled out the business prospectus she'd spent most of the night working on. She passed him the copy as she continued.

"I don't plan to just pitch myself today, Darryl. I plan to pitch us, as a team. This has really been weighing on me and what I realize is that I can't imagine working on any massive project without you."

He lifted his eyes to hers and then dropped them back down to the document in his hand. "Charles-Boudreaux Designs & Engineering?"

"It sounded better than Boudreaux-Charles Designs. But I'm open to suggestions."

Darryl continued to read, not saying anything, and Camryn's nerves kicked back into gear. She pleaded her case.

"I needed to partner with the best engineer in the industry, especially if I'm going to be building here in Dubai. The fact that I'm going to be married to the best engineer out here was just a perk."

He nodded his head slowly. "And what about Charles & Charles Architecture? Don't you think your father might have some issues with this?"

"I'm planning on doing both and my father fully supports the idea. I look at this as a means of diversification. Our collaborating on joint projects won't stop either of us from continuing to do work on individual ventures when they arise."

"Does my brother Mason know he's on the board of directors?"

"He's very excited."

Darryl laughed. "I'm sure he is."

"Surprise!" Camryn said facetiously. "So, what do you think?"

He shook his head from side to side. "I think, my darling, that I can quickly get used to the idea of being CEO of my own company!"

Camryn grinned. "If I say so myself, sir, I think you're going to be a brilliant corporate leader!"

Hours later Camryn could barely contain her excitement. The morning had gone better than she could have ever planned. Her designs had been on point, clearly capturing the attention of the sheikh and his staff. They'd asked some hard questions and she'd answered easily. She lived and breathed her work and there was no denying she was clearly talented.

Darryl was excited by her exuberance. Her enthusiasm reminded him of the first time she presented her vision to him and his brother. He'd been a hard taskmaster the way he had challenged her, and just like with him, everything they'd thrown at her, she'd given it back in spades. Throwing in his two cents about the safety issues had been the icing on the cake for their presentation.

She suddenly jumped in her seat, the color draining from her face. "I almost forgot," Camryn exclaimed.

"What's wrong?"

"While you and the sheikh were smoking cigars together, Sami told me who our competition is."

"And?"

"And they're picking up James and Asia Landry from the airport right after they drop us off for our flight home."

Chapter 17

"I think it went really well," Asia said as she settled down in the first-class seat of the Boeing airplane.

James Landry nodded his agreement. "I was very impressed with your presentation, Asia. You did a very nice job."

"You and I make a great team, Daddy!"

James settled back in his own leather seat, closing his eyes as the plane soared through a midnight sky.

"I'm so excited!" Asia exclaimed. She was like a kid in a candy shop, the way she kept bouncing around, chattering endlessly.

Her father nodded again. "Asia, when you're focused you can accomplish almost anything you want to accomplish. You were focused and your contributions to the design and proposal were really good work. You made me very proud."

"Thank you, Daddy. It's a shame we can't win, though," she said with a deep sigh.

The man cut his eye at her, not bothering to respond.

"Camryn Charles has to win this, Daddy. She has to win this so that she can move to Dubai and be out of Darryl's life forever!"

James rolled his eyes in annoyance.

"And what if Darryl decides he wants to move to Dubai with her?"

"He'd never do that. He would never leave that family of his. I know him. I know him better than she ever will. She'll get the project and once Darryl understands that he has to leave his precious family, he will call the wedding off. I'll give him some time to adjust and then I'll reach out and just be a good friend to him. Before long, I will get my happily-ever-after."

"You have this all worked out, don't you, Asia?"

"I have to, Daddy. I have to get Darryl back."

James shook his head. "And what happens if you never get Darryl back? What if Darryl has no interest in ever getting back together with you, Asia? What then?"

Asia shrugged, having never given the thought any consideration. "Daddy, don't you want me happy?" she asked.

Her father looked at her. "Asia, you haven't figured out yet that you obsessing with Darryl Boudreaux isn't going to make you happy. You obsessing over any man will never, ever make you happy. Everyone else can see it, so I'm having a very difficult time trying to figure out where the disconnect comes from. You can never be happy chasing after a man who doesn't love you or want to be with you."

"Tch!" Asia sucked her teeth, skewing her face.

Her father continued. "Clearly, what I want for you doesn't make much difference if you don't want it for yourself, Asia. You need to want a relationship with a man who's interested in you. And that man is not that Boudreaux boy. So, until the true man of your dreams makes an appearance, you need to focus on your career."

"I'm just going to have to prove you wrong, Daddy!" she said cheerfully. "So you need to please make sure Camryn wins. You need to make sure Sheikh Muhammad just loves her work more than anyone else's."

"You know, Asia, when you asked me to get her on the list for consideration, I thought you wanted to truly compete against her. I thought you wanted to make an impression that was about your talent against her talent. What you're looking for is just downright stupid."

"Does that mean you're not going to help me anymore?"

James adjusted a pillow behind his head and pulled a blanket up over his shoulders. "It means that if Camryn Charles's design beats ours, then she did a better job than we did. What happens after that doesn't have anything at all to do with me, or you. Understand?"

Crossing her arms over her chest, Asia pouted profusely. If her father wasn't going to give her any more help, she needed to come up with a contingency plan. With James and the sheikh being friends, Asia had made her father an assortment of promises to get him to suggest Camryn as a plausible candidate for the project. It hadn't hurt that Camryn Charles had an impressive list of accomplishments under her belt. Her father's reputation in the industry had been a plus, as well, and with James Landry's recommendation Camryn making the list had been assured.

Despite her father complimenting her design, Asia hadn't put much effort or thought into it. She'd proposed an outrageous, over-the-top Mall of America–like water park extravaganza. The design was out there and she couldn't fathom anyone with any sense seriously considering it. She knew that her father was just one project shy of retirement and his concerns for her well-being would have had him saying absolutely anything.

She took a quick glance toward her father. He'd fallen asleep and was beginning to snore ever so slightly. She laid her head on his shoulder, settling down for what was left of the flight. Her father loved her and she loved him even more. She only wished she could make him see that she loved Darryl Boudreaux, too.

Camryn pulled into the driveway of the Boudreaux home. There was a line of cars parked there, and knowing that his large family was probably inside warmed her spirit.

She and Darryl had been back from Dubai for almost a month. Getting their schedules back in sync had been difficult at best the first few days but since then everything seemed on point. Darryl and the crew at Boudreaux Towers were in the last phase of completion and it was truly only a matter of days before they would officially hand Mason the keys to the door.

Darryl had moved into their new house and it was slowly becoming a home. Between movers and delivery people, they were finding a place for all their furniture.

Together they'd been navigating painters, installers, utility persons and all facets of new-home ownership.

Setting up the infrastructure for their new business had also been a pressing must-do. There'd been contracts and lawyers, bank accounts and accountants to contend with. There was the selection of board members and the first board meeting. And then Darryl had thrown in his own surprise, announcing that Charles-Boudreaux Designs & Engineering was the fourth official tenant to sign at Boudreaux Towers.

Today she was meeting Darryl's sisters. The women were headed to Pearl's Place, the area's premier bridal shop, for the final fitting of their gowns. Camryn had to admit that she'd been shirking on her bridal responsibilities. Maitlyn had been a godsend, stepping in to act as their wedding planner, but Camryn hadn't been making her job easy. There were just too many decisions that she was expected to make and she truly didn't have the energy for it all. Even Darryl had commented on her lackadaisical attitude, suggesting yet again that they postpone the wedding until things settled down some. But Camryn didn't want to postpone her wedding. She just wanted it to be over and done with so that she and Darryl could get on with their life together.

Ringing the bell, she was surprised when Darryl answered the door himself.

"Hey, what are you doing here?" Camryn asked, reaching up to kiss his lips.

He sighed. "We need to talk," he said, his somber demeanor suddenly making her nervous.

There was an eerie silence floating through the home's rooms, the usual laughter nowhere to be found.

Darryl's siblings were in the kitchen, Mason, Kendrick and Kamaya seated around their mother's kitchen table. Maitlyn stood against the back wall, her cell phone pressed to her ear. Total annoyance painted her expression. As Camryn entered the room, they all turned to stare as if she'd interrupted them talking about her.

"What's wrong?" Camryn questioned, her gaze turning back to Darryl.

"Let's go into the other room," he mumbled.

She shook her head. "No. Tell me what's wrong!"

Darryl took a deep breath. "Did you cancel the wedding venue?"

A look of astonishment crossed Camryn's face. "Of course not. Why would I cancel the venue?"

"How about the band and the florist? Did you cancel either of them?"

"Darryl, of course not! Would someone please tell me what's going on!"

Maitlyn answered as she disconnected the call. "That was the dress shop. We don't have gowns. The owner said Camryn Charles called and canceled the gowns four weeks ago."

"Why would I cancel my gown? I did not cancel my gown," Camryn stated adamantly. She was incredulous.

Darryl blew another deep sigh. "Well, it seems that someone did. In fact, someone canceled our entire wedding. And everyone we've spoken to insists they spoke to you."

Camryn shook her head. "That's ridiculous! I would not have canceled our entire wedding. How could someone do that? We're getting married in eight weeks, Darryl!"

Maitlyn shook her head. "I'm sorry but as of this moment everything you ordered, requested, reserved and purchased has been canceled. Nothing for your wedding is on schedule for your wedding date. Right now all the work we've been doing for the last few months will have to be done all over again."

Camryn dropped down onto one of the padded kitchen seats. "Who would do this to us?" she asked, looking from Darryl to his family and back. "This makes no sense to me."

Darryl glanced at Maitlyn, avoiding Camryn's stare. Maitlyn gestured for him to answer. He sighed again. "We can't prove it yet, but I think Asia might have had a hand in this," he said softly.

Maitlyn rolled her eyes. "Might? Might? I don't need any proof to know that crazy fool did this. Her signature is all over this mess!" his sister exclaimed.

Camryn bristled, her spirit suddenly flooded with rage. "Asia Landry did this to us?"

Darryl shrugged. "We don't know that yet. Right now everyone is saying that you ordered the cancellations."

"Well, you know I didn't do this, Darryl. What sense does that make?"

Darryl shook his head. "If you had called the vendors before we left for Dubai like Maitlyn had asked, we might not be dealing with this right now," he said, his offhanded comment stinging her.

"I don't believe you just said that," Camryn snapped. "I'm not marrying myself, Darryl Boudreaux. You were just as capable of calling the vendors as I was. Are you saying this is my fault because I didn't have time to make two telephone calls?"

He dropped down onto the seat beside her. "Let's not fight, Camryn. We need to figure out what we need to do to turn this mess around."

"The first thing we need to do is have Asia arrested. Have you called the police?"

"They're looking into it," Maitlyn responded.

"And my attorneys are figuring out what legal recourse against Asia you and Darryl might have," Mason noted.

"She needs to pay for this," Camryn said, clearly chagrined.

"This isn't about Asia," Darryl said, his voice raised. "Why are you worrying about Asia?"

"Why are you *not* worrying about Asia? Clearly, this is just another continuation of the problem we seem to be having with your girlfriend! Or did you forget about her slashing my tires? And what about the snakes? She's already tried to kill you. Does she need to shoot at me before you start worrying about Asia?"

Darryl scowled, biting back the retort that sat thick on his tongue. Camryn was baiting him and he refused to dignify her rant with a comment. He didn't want to fight.

Maitlyn tried to defuse the situation. "Let's all relax and just focus on getting the wedding back on track. The first thing we need to do is make sure the venue hasn't scheduled anyone else in the space and rebook that. Then we need to split up the guest list and call everyone personally to let them know the wedding is still on. We can reorder the flowers and reschedule all the vendors. I'll start making those calls this afternoon. The gowns might be a problem but if push comes to shove, we'll just have to pick something off the rack."

Camryn interrupted. "I don't want something off the rack! I ordered a Monique Lhuillier gown and that's the gown I want," she snapped.

"Really, Camryn?" Darryl snapped back. "I thought you just wanted to be married. What does it matter what you wear?"

Camryn jumped to her feet. "It matters to me," she stated, tears misting her eyes. Shaking her head, Camryn stormed out of the room. By the time Darryl caught up with her, she was getting into her car.

"Camryn, where are you going? We need to figure this out."

"You figure it out," she said. "I'm done."

"What do you mean you're done?"

"I mean I'm tired, Darryl. I'm tired of Asia Landry making our lives hell and you ignoring it like she's too fragile to deal with the consequences. She did this. You know she did this and you want to fuss me out for not making a damn phone call? Well, guess what? Now I'm not making *any* phone calls."

"I'm not ignoring it, Camryn, but what do you want me to do?"

"I want you to get mad. I want you to blame Asia. I want you to make her accountable for her actions and I want you to stop thinking that I should just let Asia slide just because you say you don't care about her anymore. I'm not letting her slide and you're just too damn passive about everything that woman does."

"What are you going to do, Camryn?"

"I would like to beat her down, that's what I would like to do. And if I run into her, I might just do that."

"You should be focusing all that energy into recovering our wedding."

"I'm not interested in doing that right now."

"So what are you saying? You don't want to get married?"

Camryn shook her head. "I am saying that right now, at this very minute, I'm angry and I don't want to deal with this."

Darryl nodded slowly. "So that's it?"

She shrugged. "Yes. I'm tired, Darryl, and I don't have anything to give you right now." She slid into the driver's seat of the vehicle and started the engine.

Taking a deep breath, Darryl closed the car door. He blew a heavy sigh. As Camryn backed out of the driveway, he turned and headed back inside the house. Neither one bothered to look back at the other.

Maitlyn was shaking her head at him. Even Kendrick's expression was telling. Mason said out loud what they were all thinking.

"Little brother, I'm no relationship expert but I'm thinking you really didn't handle this situation well."

Darryl tossed up his hands in frustration. "What was I supposed to do?"

"Not blame your fiancée, for starters," Kamaya interjected.

Maitlyn added her two cents. "Darryl, you're just like Mason. You both are forgiving to a fault. And just so *docile* about everything."

"Docile?"

"You never, ever react when things happen. Camryn needed you to react to what Asia has done to you two. Instead, you give her grief like she did something wrong."

Kamaya was nodding her head. "Personally, if I were Camryn, I would never speak to you again. And I definitely wouldn't marry your behind."

Darryl cut a narrowed eye at his sister. Kendrick shrugged his shoulders.

Mason shook his head from side to side. "It's not that bad, Darryl. She's angry right now but it won't last. Your woman has a lot of spirit and she doesn't take things lightly. You are just like me. And like Senior. We assess the pros and cons of everything and we respond based on what's best for the situation. Women are more excitable. Between their emotions and their hormones, they react first and think about everything afterward."

"It has nothing to do with our hormones!" Maitlyn chimed.

Mason and Kendrick laughed. Kamaya scowled.

Darryl sighed deeply, his head waving from side to side. He met his sister's critical stare. "Maitlyn, can you salvage my wedding?"

"Do you have a bride?" she asked sarcastically.

"I'll make things right with Camryn."

Maitlyn paused, meeting his pleading gaze. "Then I'll help with the rest."

"We all will," Kamaya added, their brothers nodding in agreement.

Darryl smiled ever so slightly. "What about her gown? She has to have that gown."

Maitlyn nodded. "I'll make some calls. You will

probably be paying a premium on such short notice but it's not impossible."

"Whatever it costs," Darryl professed. "Just please, make it happen."

Camryn had lost count of the number of times Darryl had called her cell phone. Each call had gone directly to her voice mail, with him leaving a message that he was sorry, he loved her and he needed to speak with her. She wasn't, however, in the mood for conversation. She was still angry, furious with the entire situation. She was also frustrated that she was feeling so out of control. And hurt. Darryl's ambivalence had actually hurt her feelings.

She sighed heavily as she popped the lid on her plastic container and reached for one of the pecan praline candies inside. Since that first batch, Darryl had kept her in pecan praline candy. She'd been fascinated the first time she'd watched him cook a pan of the sweet confection. She had teased him repeatedly about faking it, passing off someone else's cooking as his own. To prove her wrong he had steered her into the kitchen, settling her comfortably at the oversize counter to watch him in action.

He had mixed brown sugar, heavy cream, butter and a pinch of baking soda together in a heavy saucepan. As the mixture simmered on the stove, Darryl had stirred it until it reached the perfect consistency, looking creamy and cloudy, and then he'd thrown in the pecans. With an ice cream scoop he'd dropped the treats onto parchment paper to cool.

He'd been sexy as hell as he'd teased her with the

decadent concoction, allowing her to lick the treat from his fingers. He'd brushed a damp finger coated with the raw sugar over her top lip and then he'd kissed her, both savoring the sweetness. As the mixture had thickened he'd pulled small spoonfuls out to taste, and once they were cooled, he'd dropped the treat onto her tongue. That first batch had almost failed when the two had become distracted with tasting each other. Camryn almost orgasmed at the memory.

She crossed her legs, sitting Indian-style beneath the desk in her father's office. She hadn't gone home, knowing Darryl would look for her there first. She had also avoided her own office, figuring that was the next likely place he'd think to look for her. Instead, she'd gone to her father's, seeking sanctuary in the familiar comforts of her childhood home. With Kenneth Charles being out of town, there was no way he could confirm or deny her whereabouts.

Camryn took a deep breath. As a little girl, she had played beneath her father's desk. It had been her favorite spot in the whole house. Supplied with crayons and coloring paper, she'd drawn pretty buildings just like her daddy. Her father had indulged every one of her wishes, from pen and paper to Popsicle sticks and Lego blocks. For each building her father had designed, she had designed two. Being as good an architect as her daddy had been the only thing she had ever aspired to. Until Darryl.

Since meeting Darryl, Camryn had aspired to also be a great partner and an even better friend. Becoming Darryl's wife, bearing his children and growing old with him would be proof of her success. And Asia Landry was trying hard to stand in her way. Camryn saw it. She had no understanding of why Darryl couldn't. She popped another candy into her mouth, fighting back the tears that pressed hot against the backs of her eyelids.

After the third piece of confection, Camryn felt her ire subsiding. By the fifth piece, she was missing Darryl, wishing that she were in his arms because she felt safe there. She reached for her cell phone, checking her missed calls. Her mailbox was full, Darryl having left his last message three hours earlier.

Chapter 18

He'd been tossing from side to side ever since he'd lain down for the night, finally giving up on finding Camryn. He'd been blowing up her telephone all day and she had not bothered to return one of his calls. For her to completely shut herself off told him that she was beyond angry with him. Camryn usually enjoyed a good fight and from the moment they'd met, they'd had one or two doozies. But Camryn also enjoyed the making up, and since they'd committed to each other, she'd been adamant that they would never go to bed angry. And now here he was, going to bed alone, no making up in sight.

His cell phone rested on the pillow beside him. He took a quick glance, hoping against all odds that she had at least sent him a text to say that she was okay. But the screen was blank—no text, no voice mail, no nothing from her. He shook his head and stared up toward the ceiling.

It was truly working his spirit to have Camryn so angry at him, and particularly over some other woman. It worked his spirit because there was no other woman he would ever allow to come between the two of them. There was no other woman who could ever have his heart the way Camryn had his heart, most especially not a woman like Asia Landry. Clearly, he'd not done a good job ensuring that Camryn knew that.

Darryl suddenly sat straight up in the bed. It was the second time in a ten-minute span that he'd been certain that he'd heard something. The first time he'd attributed it to a new house settling, the creaks and squeaks happening as wood expanded and shrank. But this time he was less concerned about it being the house itself and more concerned with someone else being in the house with him.

Reaching over to the nightstand, he turned on the light. Bright rays illuminated the roomy space. Camryn had picked out the lamps, contemporary table fixtures with shades made of paper and raw cotton. He'd initially balked at the price and then she'd set them in place, turning on the bulbs. They cast just enough light around the room to create a seductive ambiance. Darryl smiled as he reflected back to the moment when he'd been impressed.

Camryn had turned on the lights as he'd lain across the bed. As he lay watching, she'd slowly done a seductive striptease. With her body shadowed against the back wall, she'd danced out of her clothes. Her blouse had come off first, and then the pencil skirt she'd been wearing. Garters had held up her thigh-high stockings, and her bra and panties had been sheer white lace and silk. She'd crawled across the bed and had stood above him, the light accenting the warmth of her complexion. Standing atop the mattress, her body straddled above his, Camryn had done a slow gyration out of her remaining clothes and then beneath the shimmer of that light they had made the sweetest love. Reflecting back had incited a raging erection between his legs and Darryl resisted the urge to palm his hand across his crotch. His organ twitched in his shorts and he knew that if he didn't get some release, he could possibly blow his load down his leg without even touching himself.

The sound of the hardwood floors creaking beneath someone's feet pulled him back to the moment. Lifting himself from the bed, he reached behind the nightstand for the 12-gauge he kept hidden from view. As he turned toward the door, Camryn suddenly stepped through it. Meeting her gaze, he breathed a deep sigh.

"Hey," he said softly.

The young woman smiled, a gentle bend to her luscious mouth. She pointed at the weapon in his hands. "Are you going to shoot some bad guys?"

"I was about to defend our home against an intruder," he answered as he returned the shotgun to its hiding spot. "How did you get in?"

"I'd taken the spare key to make copies, remember?"

Darryl nodded his head. He hadn't remembered.

Camryn shrugged her shoulders, meeting his eyes. "I couldn't sleep."

"I'm glad."

"That's not nice."

He shrugged. "I'm glad that you couldn't go to sleep mad at me."

She smiled ever so sweetly, her gaze still connected to his deep stare.

"I'm sorry," Darryl said quietly. "And I want you to know that I was angry with Asia. I was pissed that she would do what she did. But I took my frustrations out on you and I apologize for that."

"One day I'm going to get you to hoop and holler when you're mad about something. You can't be so calm and collected all the time."

"One day," Darryl said with a chuckle.

They continued to stare at each other.

"Do you still want to marry me?" Camryn said.

Darryl smiled. "More than you know. But I thought I'd be the one asking that question first."

"So what are you waiting for?"

He paused, suddenly fighting back his emotion. Tears misted his eyes. "Do you still want to marry me, Camryn?" Darryl asked.

Without a second's hesitation she hurried into the room and stepped swiftly into his arms. She moved against him, her mouth lifting to his, and she kissed him very softly on the lips. It was heaven. Wrapping his arms around her, Darryl pulled her tightly to him, kissing her over and over again. He nuzzled his face against hers, his cheek caressing her cheek gently. He couldn't begin to express just how much he'd missed her. He sighed, gratitude filling his spirit as he whispered a prayer of thanks.

"We don't have to have a wedding," Camryn whispered. "I'd be happy if we went down to town hall in our pajamas. I just want to be your wife."

Darryl nodded with understanding. "And I will be

you husband. But you're going to get your dream wedding, baby. I wouldn't have it any other way."

"My dress, too?" Camryn asked teasingly.

Darryl chuckled. "Your dress, too!"

After hours of conversation, the two came to an understanding about each other's expectations and desires. Camryn had insisted on a game plan to deal with the issues between them and Darryl had been happy to oblige her. He'd also been sensitive to her shutting down and putting distance between them and she had promised to never again doubt his love for her. Both knew that without a line of communication there would be little they could accomplish as a team. And they were a team, partnering in business and in life. Whatever the challenges, they were committed to facing them together.

He made love to her that night. He made love to her and Camryn loved him back as if both their lives depended on it. Back in Darryl's arms, she slept well, once again feeling safe and secure. And Darryl couldn't remember ever being so happy.

They slept late the next morning, awakening in a tangle of flesh and limbs. Rising first, Camryn splashed water on her face and brushed her teeth. Darryl entered the bathroom as she stood staring at her reflection in the large mirror. He relieved himself in the commode, then washed his own face and rinsed his mouth out. Both returned to the bed and Darryl stacked the pillows beneath his head as he pulled Camryn to him. She rested her head on his chest, pressing a palm against his abdomen.

"Good morning, Mr. Boudreaux."

"Good morning, Ms. Charles," Darryl answered.

"How did you sleep?"

He hugged her closer. "I slept like a baby. How about you?"

"Me too!"

"We need to get up," Darryl professed.

Camryn shrugged. "Do we?"

He chuckled softly. "At some point!"

"But not right now," she said as she kissed his warm flesh, drawing random circles against his skin.

Darryl tipped her face to his with his hand, cupping his fingers beneath her chin. He kissed her deeply, sucking her lower lip in between his own lips, his tongue gliding over it, down between her lip and teeth, then into her mouth to engage her tongue. He sucked her entire upper lip in between his own, his tongue continuing to probe her mouth excitedly, sliding deeply into the oral cavity and against her tongue. She tasted like the minty mouthwash and toothpaste they'd used. Her lips were soft and delicate and the sweetness of them had him shivering with desire. When Darryl finally broke the kiss, they were both panting heavily.

"It's definitely a good morning," Camryn muttered. She snuggled closer against him.

Darryl traced his hand across her upper torso, grazing her shoulders and down the length of her arm. His fingers entwining with hers, he pulled her hand to his lips and gently kissed her palm and each one of her fingers. Camryn tilted her face back to his and gently kissed him on each of his cheeks. She waited a heartbeat and then kissed him full on the lips again, nudging her body closer to his as she did.

The gentleness of the kiss quickly progressed from gentle to ardent. She felt him brush his tongue against her lips and with automatic reflex she opened her mouth to greet it with her own. Her nipples hardened between them, pressing hard against the tight line of his chest. When he pulled his mouth from her mouth, her lips were still tingling from the heat. Camryn knew that the memory of Darryl's lips would be with her for the rest of her day. An involuntary smile filled her face at the thought.

She slid farther into his arms and they continued to share light butterfly kisses and the gentle touch of each other's hands. Up and down their respective bodies they teased and explored each other's hidden treasures. Camryn suddenly let out a loud gasp as Darryl's hand ventured between her legs, coming to rest on her bare mound. His touch sent an erotic surge rippling through her.

Reaching between them, Camryn ran her index finger along his rising length, gently tapping against his shaft. When she swirled the pad of her finger slowly across the head, it made him gasp, sucking air in swiftly as his body tingled with pleasure. In response he trailed his tongue over the curve of her ear and left a path of damp kisses as Camryn leaned her neck toward him.

Darryl rolled himself forward until he was resting above her, kissing her deeply. Kisses that Camryn returned with equal passion as her small hands trailed the length of his back. His fingers danced a pathway from her neck across her brown flesh to the bountiful breast, and where his fingers danced, his lips followed.

His touch was tender and determined, marking her with every ounce of love he had for her.

Camryn moaned appreciatively as Darryl's mouth latched around her right nipple, his tongue darting playfully across the rock hard treat as his fingers tugged and kneaded the other. He alternated between the two, the demonstrative gestures causing her feminine spirit to pulse with a vengeance. Camryn cried out softly as she felt the warmth of his mouth becoming heated against her flesh. Darryl paused, shifting his gaze to her face, wanting to admire the lust-filled glow that painted her expression. Her breathing was coming in short, easy gasps as he returned his attention to her breasts, his tongue running around the dark circle, tickling the swollen nipple. He softly squeezed the fullness of her, complementing the ripples of joy his mouth produced. He shifted to the identical mound on the other side, lavishing it with equal attention as he moved back and forth, both delighting in the exhilaration.

Camryn was heated, perspiration beading in all of her creases. Darryl's weight felt good to her, his body pressed above hers. She opened her legs, spreading herself wide in invitation. Her moans were coming quicker and in greater volume.

Camryn leaned to murmur in Darryl's ear. "I need to feel you inside me," she whispered anxiously.

Darryl kissed his way back to her mouth, his hands still cradling each of her breasts. He was heavy, his body pressing her tight to the mattress. The heat and pressure felt incredible, the phenomenal pleasure intense.

He reclaimed her mouth, his lips skating over hers as

he entered her easily, sliding his engorged member deep into her folds. He stroked her over and over again, gliding in and out of her as her muscles tightened sweetly around him. Her insides were hot and throbbing, pulsing wildly around his hardness. He was covered in her nectar, her moisture flooding between them as he penetrated her in a mix of slow and rapid movement.

Camryn let out a long low sigh as she savored the sweetness of their connection. Her eyes were closed, her head thrown back against the pillows as the first waves of passion washed over her. Her body quaked with desire as she grabbed the sheet beneath her, bunching it in her hand. Darryl felt her coming, her muscles so tight around his that she drew him in deeper and deeper with each thrust. He was covered in sweat, unsuccessful in his efforts to hold back. The forces raging across his flesh refused to let either of them go and when Camryn screamed, her orgasm inciting his, Darryl screamed with her. It was the sweetest surrender for them both.

Chapter 19

With Christmas only days away and her wedding happening in just over a week, Camryn couldn't believe that she and Darryl were headed to London to meet with Sheikh Muhammad. The sheikh had requested the meeting just hours earlier, this time sending his own private aircraft, a massive Boeing 747, to transport them. London was deemed a convenient location since the junior wife wanted to do her holiday shopping at Harrods. Despite the inconvenience of it all, Camryn had found the prospect of shopping at Harrods intriguing, as well.

She flipped through her copy of the formal prospectus that she'd submitted to the monarch, revisiting her notes and concerns to ensure she was well informed for the meeting. Darryl dropped his hand on top of hers and gently squeezed her fingers.

"Are you excited?" Darryl asked, having already reviewed his own notes.

Camryn shrugged. "To be honest, I'm not sure. I honestly don't know if I'm ready for all the change that will have to take place if he awards us the project."

"Well, baby, you better get ready because I don't think he's flying us to London to *not* award us the project."

"You've got a point," she said nonchalantly as she shifted in her seat.

Darryl laughed. "I'm impressed with how calm you are!"

"I can't afford to be nervous. If I let my nerves get to me, I might make a mistake."

Darryl leaned to kiss her cheek. "You won't make a mistake."

Camryn shifted forward in her seat, turning to stare at the man. "What about you, Darryl? You're concerned about me but are you nervous?"

"Hell, yeah! My knees haven't stopped shaking since we got the call from Sheikh Muhammad this morning."

"It is pretty intimidating the way he calls and commands your presence when he wants you."

"He's a powerful man and powerful men have their own way of doing things."

"I'm discovering that," she said, brushing a finger down the side of his face, her eyebrows raised.

Darryl laughed again. "What are you trying to say?"

"I'm saying that it does a body good to know a powerful man. And it's even better when you're in love with one." Her seductive smile was enticing.

Darryl smiled with her, reaching for her hand a second time. "No matter what happens, Camryn, I love me some you, too."

* * *

London was dazzling. After another exciting day Camryn and Darryl returned to their hotel room at Boudreaux Hotel & Resort London, one of the hotels his brother Mason had founded. They were ready for hot showers and some serious sleep. After closing and locking the door to their suite, Darryl pulled his jacket off and his turtleneck sweater up and over his head and dropped both to the floor. Moving behind him, Camryn retrieved his garments and followed him from the living space into the bedroom, where she hung them in the closet. She shook her head at him and he smiled, shrugging his shoulders in apology.

"I cannot believe what a wonderful time I'm having!" Camryn exclaimed as Darryl removed the rest of his clothing.

He nodded in agreement. "Even after everything that's happened?" he questioned as he leaned to kiss her forehead.

"Most especially after everything that's happened," Camryn answered. A sly smile illuminated her face as she brushed her hand across his chest.

Darryl moved in the direction of the hotel's bathroom and the shower. "We have a long day tomorrow," he said, tossing the comment over his wide shoulder.

"You still haven't told me what we're doing tomorrow!"

Darryl grinned, pausing in the doorway. "I know. But trust me. It's going to be a very long day," he reiterated.

She shook her head as he disappeared inside the bathroom, the door closing just a fraction behind him.

Minutes later she could hear the water running and Darryl singing Christmas carols loudly. Laughing to herself, Camryn kicked off her shoes and slipped out of her own clothes. She tossed them over an upholstered chair and slid her body across the bed. Sprawling out comfortably in the center of the mattress, she let out a deep breath. Darryl's rich baritone voice rang merrily through the room, bringing a bright smile to her face.

Had someone told her that she and Darryl would still be in London on Christmas Eve, she would have told them they were crazy. But here they were on Christmas Eve, still enjoying London.

The decision had been all Darryl's and it had been impulsive and spontaneous. Camryn had balked at first, insisting they had too much to do back home. Darryl had responded with a resounding "To hell with it," insisting that they both needed a break and a break was what they were going to have. She was thankful for it.

Despite the short days and dreary weather, exploring London over the holidays definitely had perks. They'd spent the morning at Trafalgar Square, taking photographs of the massive holiday tree. Then Darryl had insisted on them hitting the outdoor ice rinks for skating. At the Somerset House they'd glided on blades alongside the facade of the grand neoclassical building and she couldn't remember the last time she'd had so much fun. Between spinning freely in Darryl's arms, falling flat on her behind and laughing hysterically with him when he'd tumbled down on top of her, the two had had the best time together. Afterward they'd relaxed along the river Thames at the Mayflower pub, enjoying an early meal of beer-battered haddock, chips and mushy peas. By the second pint of ale, Camryn wasn't thinking about anything or anyone except herself and Darryl. She grinned as she rolled over onto her side, thinking back on her trip.

Their morning arrival in London had been event filled. As they'd checked into the hotel, Asia and James Landry had been checking in, as well. Darryl had greeted the old man politely.

"Mr. Landry, how are you, sir?"

"Darryl, it's good to see you, son. And I'm very well. These long flights are starting to wear me down, though."

Darryl nodded in agreement. "They can be quite taxing."

"Of course, it helps to fly first class," Asia interjected as she looped an arm through her father's. "Isn't that right, Daddy?" She cut an eye at Camryn before turning her attention back to the handsome man. "Hello, Darryl," she said sweetly.

Darryl tossed her a quick nod of his head. "Asia." Darryl slipped an arm around Camryn's waist, drawing her to him. "Mr. Landry, let me introduce you to my fiancée. This is Camryn Charles. Camryn, Mr. James Landry."

Camryn extended a manicured hand. "It's a pleasure to meet you, Mr. Landry. My father speaks quite highly of you, sir."

"It's very nice to finally meet you, Ms. Charles. I am a big admirer of yours. How is Kenneth?"

"He's doing very well. Thank you for asking."

The man looked from her to Darryl and back. "And congratulations to you both. When is the wedding?"

Darryl and Camryn responded simultaneously.

"New Year's Eve."

"December 31."

Asia rolled her eyes, her face twisted in annoyance. "Well, that's so soon! It must have been hard to pull all those plans together on such short notice. Let's hope it all turns out well," she said facetiously.

Her malevolent smile made Darryl cringe. Camryn's own smile back was just as hostile and her eyes were narrowed as she glared at the other woman.

"Well, again, congratulations and happy holidays to you," the patriarch chimed as he pulled Asia along behind him, leading her to the bank of elevators that led to the upper rooms.

Darryl and Camryn tossed each other a look. She shrugged, pushing her shoulders skyward.

"Well," Darryl said, "maybe the sheikh did fly us all the way to London to tell us we didn't get the job!"

Camryn laughed. "Aren't you proud of me? I didn't even think about punching her in her face."

"Very proud, baby!" Darryl grinned. "Very proud."

Camryn sighed deeply at the memory. She rolled back to her other side, Darryl's singing pulling her back to the moment. It was clear that his spirit was lifted and in that moment everything in his world was bringing him joy and happiness. He broke out into another chorus of "Silver Bells" and Camryn's mouth lifted upward. Everything about the man made her smile.

The water felt good falling down against his shoulders and chest. Darryl enjoyed the flush of warm air and the heated spray washing over his body. He felt relaxed, not an ounce of tension in any of his muscles. He tilted his head forward into the spray, the warm water raining down over his head.

He and Camryn had been moving nonstop since arriving in London. There had been meetings with the sheikh and his people, dinner with the monarch and his wife, an encounter or two with Asia and her father, and then a much-needed break from all of it.

He had been thoroughly enjoying their mini vacation. The first day, he had taken her to the Hyde Park Winter Wonderland. They'd ridden a Ferris wheel and a carousel, seen a circus show, walked through the German market and Bavarian Village, and wasted much money on kitschy gifts for the family.

On the second day, he'd insisted on all inside activities and they had toured the British Museum and the National Portrait Gallery. Theater season was also in high gear in London, so they'd seen *The Phantom of the Opera* at Her Majesty's Theatre. When he'd discovered that Camryn liked big glitzy productions, he'd finagled tickets to a late-night performance of Cirque du Soleil at the grand, red-velvet-draped Royal Albert Hall. In between it all they had nibbled their way through Borough Market, enjoying mulled wine, pudding, mince pie and other seasonal treats. The second day had been a good day.

Today, after spending the afternoon ice-skating, Darryl had to finally admit that he was officially exhausted. And they still had Christmas Day ahead of them. He sighed, closing his eyes tightly. After taking a moment to catch his breath, he whispered a quick prayer and then started singing.

Minutes later Camryn's voice broke through the moment.

"Are you going to leave me any hot water?" she asked as she stepped into the shower with him, leaning her naked body against his back.

Turning an about-face, Darryl wrapped his arms around her and spun her into the water. He leaned to kiss her lips, his mouth skating easily over hers.

"I'm done," Darryl said. "I was just about to get out."

Camryn chuckled softly. "You looked like it, too."

He tapped her on the bottom, the smack resonating loudly in the enclosed space.

"Ohhh," Camryn said with a grin. "You got me all tingly!"

He shook his head. "Finish your shower and come to bed. Let me see if I can't do something about that tingling for you!" he said with another slap on her buttock.

"Ouch!" she said, rubbing the sting out of her flesh.

She watched as Darryl eased his way out of the shower, reaching for one of the plush white towels to wrap around his waist. Closing the bathroom door securely behind him, he left her to her own devices.

As he closed the door, Darryl heard his cell phone ringing against the dresser top. Noting the caller ID, he was grateful for the timing. He took a quick glance over his shoulder before answering the call.

"Hello?"

Maitlyn greeted him cheerfully. "Hey there! We just landed."

Darryl nodded his head into the receiver, forgetting

that she couldn't see him on the other end. A wide smile pulled at his full lips. "Did you all have a good flight?"

"We did. Does she suspect anything?"

Darryl grinned. "No, Camryn doesn't suspect a thing!"

Chapter 20

Camryn could hear a telephone ringing. It jangled harshly, sounding as if it were off in the distance somewhere moving toward her fast. The fog in her head seemed to be lifting slowly as that ringing telephone got louder and louder. She reached her hand across the bed for Darryl, mumbling for him to make the ringing stop, but then realized he wasn't there. Lifting herself upright in the bed, Camryn suddenly realized that Darryl was nowhere to be found. The hotel room telephone was still ringing.

"Hello?"

"Merry Christmas, sleepy-head!" Darryl chimed into his end of the receiver.

"Merry Christmas! What time is it?"

"Almost two o'clock. You've slept half the day away."

Camryn reached for her cell phone, eyeing the digital readout. "Why didn't you wake me up?"

"Because you are so beautiful when you're snoring!"

Camryn shook her head. "Where are you?"

"Getting ready for our big day," Darryl said, joy resonating in his tone.

"Darryl Boudreaux, what are you up to?"

There was a knock on the bedroom door. A wave of panic suddenly swept over Camryn. She whispered loudly into the receiver. "Darryl, someone's in the living room. If it's not you, who is it?" she asked as she pulled the bedsheets up over her nakedness.

Darryl laughed. "It's probably Maitlyn."

"Maitlyn? What is your sister doing—?"

The knock sounded a second time, interrupting her question.

"You better let her in before she breaks down the door," Darryl said, laughing. "Trust me. It's all going to be okay."

"Darryl, I don't understand. What's going on?"

"Open the door. Maitlyn will explain everything. I love you, baby!" he said as he disconnected the call.

"Just a minute!" Camryn called out as she threw her legs off the side of the bed and grabbed her silk bathrobe. She yanked a hand through her tangled curls, pulling the strands into a loose bun on top of her head. Moving to the door, she pulled it open, and just as Darryl had said, Maitlyn was standing on the other side.

"Merry Christmas!" Darryl's sister said excitedly.

Camryn's face was awash with confusion. "Maitlyn, what's going on?"

Maitlyn laughed as she took a quick glance down to the watch on her wrist. She motioned for Camryn to follow her into the other room. "What's going on is you are getting married today!"

"What?" Her expression was incredulous as she looked around the living space. All of Darryl's sisters were waiting for her, their wide smiles greeting her warmly.

"Merry Christmas!" Tarah cheered, rushing to give her a big hug.

"Happy holiday!" Kamaya added.

Camryn looked overwhelmed, widening her eyes like a deer caught in headlights. She looked from one woman to the next, noting the three new faces that she didn't recognize. The questioning look in her eyes moved them to introduce themselves.

Phaedra Stallion-Boudreaux waved her hand from her seat on the sofa. "It's so nice to meet you. I'm Mason's wife, Phaedra," she said warmly. "Congratulations!"

"And I'm Dahlia, Guy's wife!" Dahlia Morrow-Boudreaux introduced herself.

Katrina Stallion stepped forward, extending her hand in greeting. "And I'm Darryl's sister Katrina. Welcome to the family!"

"Hi!" Camryn said as Katrina leaned in to give her a warm embrace. "And thank you." Her eyes misted with tears. "Would one of you please tell me what's going on?"

They all laughed.

Maitlyn explained. "Darryl decided that since you both wanted a simple ceremony with just the family, there was no reason you couldn't have the ceremony here in London. So we all flew in and in exactly four hours, at six o'clock tonight, you will be getting married in the Garden banquet room, and then we'll all celebrate by having Christmas dinner. Until then, we have a team of stylists coming to do manicures, pedicures, hair and makeup. And we're all going to hang out, drink champagne and enjoy the pampering." She pointed to the buffet of fresh fruits, pastries and cheeses that was laid out for them.

Camryn shook her head in complete awe. "What about my father and brother?"

"Mr. Charles and Carson are hanging out with the men," Kamaya answered.

"It's Christmas, so they can't get in too much trouble!" Maitlyn exclaimed.

"And everything we planned for next week? What's going to happen?" Camryn asked.

Maitlyn waved her index finger. "Oh, you're still having a New Year's reception. Those plans have not changed, no matter what Asia might have tried to do," she said with a wry laugh.

Camryn laughed with her.

"What did Asia do?" Katrina asked.

"You would not believe—" Maitlyn started before being interrupted. There was a knock on the main door and Tarah moved to open it. Katherine Boudreaux stood on the other side, a large dress bag in her hands.

"Hi, Mom!" the girls all chimed.

"Merry Christmas, Mrs. Boudreaux," Camryn said as Katherine passed the bag to Maitlyn and moved to hug Camryn tightly.

"Were you surprised, baby?" she asked.

Camryn nodded. "I'm in shock, actually."

Katherine laughed. "I just think it's all so exciting!" she exclaimed.

Kamaya gestured toward the bag in Maitlyn's hands. "Darryl wanted us to give you your Christmas present," she said.

Maitlyn held the bag out toward Camryn, grinning widely. Katrina moved in behind Katherine, wrapping her arms around her mother's neck. Tarah jumped up and down excitedly beside them as Kamaya and Phaedra both moved in closer to get a better view.

"Open it!" Kamaya said.

Camryn looked from woman to woman as she stepped forward and slowly pulled down the bag's zipper. As it slid low, her Monique Lhuillier gown came into view. The tears that had previously misted Camryn's eyes suddenly dropped past her lashes, rolling over her cheeks.

From the designer's spring collection, the dress was called Poet, and it was extraordinary beyond words. Camryn lifted the white silk double-layered Chantilly lace sheath dress from the bag, her hand passing gently over the embellished bateau neck and back. It was her dream come true.

"Darryl was adamant that you have your gown," Maitlyn said. "You two put me through some things, I'm here to tell you!"

Tarah laughed. "We all know that if we need it done, Maitlyn's the one to call."

Katherine shook her head. "Y'all need to do some things on your own. I swear, your sister doesn't get a break. It's like you kids can't wipe your butts without asking Maitlyn what kind of toilet tissue to use."

Katrina laughed. "Have we gotten that bad, Mama?"

Katherine rolled her eyes, her head bobbing up and down.

Tarah shrugged. "She shouldn't be so darn good at everything," she said.

Maitlyn shook her head. "It's not that bad. And I just got a very nice break, thank you very much. I had a great time on my cruise."

"That's 'cause she met a man!" Tarah exclaimed.

Everyone in the room turned to look at Maitlyn. Her eyes widened at the sudden attention. She gave Tarah an evil eye. "Today is not about me. We're here to support Camryn," she said through clenched teeth.

Camryn laughed. "I want to know about your new man, too," she said with a giggle.

Maitlyn tossed her the same evil look she'd just given her baby sister. "We're going to change the subject now," she said. "Let me go hang your dress up for you."

The women laughed and chattered easily amongst themselves. After downing a bowl of fruit and a cup of coffee, Camryn excused herself, moving back into the bedroom. Sitting on the edge of the mattress, she depressed the speed-dial number on her cell phone, calling Darryl's phone. He answered on the first ring.

"Hey, baby! Are you okay?"

"You are truly something else, Darryl Boudreaux!"

"You're not upset, are you?"

"Why would I be upset? The man I love wants to marry me!"

"Yes, I do! And before Christmas is over you'll be Mrs. Camryn Boudreaux and I'll be the happiest man in the world!"

Camryn grinned into the receiver. "This is the best Christmas I could have ever had!"

"Look at him! Look at him!" Guy Boudreaux teased, pointing at his brother.

Kendrick laughed. "He's just as whipped as you and Mason are and he hasn't even said 'I do' yet!"

"I resemble that," Mason said. "And I'm not ashamed to admit it!"

The men in the room laughed.

"That's the problem with you young boys today," Kenneth Charles noted. "You think if your woman's in charge, it makes you less of a man."

"That's right," Senior said, cosigning. "I'm the first one to admit that my wife wears the pants in our home and I'm still a man."

Kenneth nodded. "The trick is knowing the difference between what's true and what your woman wants to believe. Most women need to believe they're in charge, so you roll with it. It keeps the peace while you go on and do your thing. That's what a real man does."

"Man's got to have peace in his home," Senior added.

Darryl and his brothers glanced at each other, all of them chuckling beneath their breaths.

Camryn's twin brother, Carson, rolled his eyes. "Personally, I don't plan to get married anytime soon. Too many women out here for me to be taking myself off the market."

Darryl's brother Donovan reached out to slap Carson's palm. "That's what I'm saying."

Darryl's brother-in-law Matthew Stallion shook his head. "You young boys just don't have a clue. If you find the right woman, you won't even think about being on the market."

"I've found the right woman," Matthew's stepson and Darryl's nephew, Collin Broomes, interjected. "My girl's hot."

"Yeah, what's this I hear about you and your girl?" Darryl demanded. "You better be protecting yourself."

Collin blushed, heat flooding his cheeks.

"I've told him," Matthew added as he dropped a hand on his stepson's shoulder. "You can't be too safe these days. He should be practicing abstinence, is what he should be doing."

Donovan laughed. "Good luck with that!"

"Damn kids today are too fast," Senior interjected. "You tell 'em to wait until marriage and they look at you like you're crazy."

Kenneth nodded his gray head in agreement. The Boudreaux sons shifted their gazes from one to another, none bothering to comment.

"Did you wait until marriage, Uncle Darryl?" Collin asked, a smug grin pulling at the young boy's mouth.

Kendrick laughed, slapping hands with Donovan.

"Of course!" Darryl exclaimed. He crossed to the other side of the room, playfully slapping the boy in the back of the head as he moved to the table of refreshments to retrieve a croissant.

"Ouch!"

Darryl and his brothers laughed. The two patriarchs both shook their heads.

Mason quickly changed the subject. "So, you haven't told us. What happened with the Dubai project?"

Darryl took a seat on the sofa. "We didn't get it," he

said casually. "The James Landry Group had the winning bid."

"You're kidding me," Mason said. "Asia Landry's design beat Camryn's?"

Darryl nodded. "Yes, sir."

"I'm sorry to hear that," Mason intoned.

"Don't be. We will still be working for the royal family. The sheikh wants to build Camryn's design in Bahrain. So we'll be doing it, we just won't be doing it in Dubai. And we'll be working for him in the United States, as well."

"How's that?" Carson asked.

"The sheikh has purchased a substantial amount of property in the United States—in Georgia and in Texas. He's hired us to design two equestrian centers for him. We'll also be doing one here in London, one in Greece and another in Riyadh. He chose Camryn because of her passion for horses."

Matthew shifted forward in his seat. "Now, that's interesting," he said. "If there's a way that Briscoe Ranch and Stallion Enterprises can partner on that in some way, I'd love to discuss the opportunity with you."

Mason nodded. "Matthew's a horseman himself. You have a horse that's competing for the Triple Crown this year, don't you, Matthew?"

His brother-in-law nodded. "We do. He was a gift for Katrina. He's a three-year-old thoroughbred named Fair Justice. We have high hopes for him."

"We should definitely talk," Darryl said. "After my honeymoon, of course."

"I have a question," Kendrick said, raising his hand

as if he were in school. "How did that crazy ex take the news of your pending nuptials?" the man asked.

Darryl took a deep breath. "You mean you really didn't hear?"

His brothers shook their heads from side to side.

Darryl paused, reflecting back on their last encounter with Asia and her father. The sheikh had wasted no time informing them that their bid was no longer under consideration. It was then that he'd presented the offer for their newly formed company to design and build a brand of multipurpose equestrian centers. The main purpose of each facility was the accommodation, training and competition of equids. They would each have commercial operations that included boarding stables and a livery yard. There would also be complementary services such as a riding school, farriers, vet services and tack shops.

The prospect of all she could do excited Camryn. And that excitement carried them out of their meeting down to the hotel's lobby, where they ran right into Asia and her father for the second time.

James Landry and his daughter were in deep conversation, Asia obviously not happy. Both Camryn and Darryl thought her behavior odd, with her having just acquired one of the biggest international contracts ever. But clearly Asia was unhappy and James didn't seem at all concerned.

"What do you think is going on with them?" Camryn wondered.

Darryl shrugged. "Who knows! As long as she doesn't bother us, I couldn't care less."

"Not that I really want to, but we should go congrat-
ulate them," Camryn said.

Darryl nodded and they walked over to offer their
commendation.

"Thank you," James said, shaking Darryl's hand.

"You both must be very excited," Camryn interjected
politely.

Asia glared. Rising suddenly, she turned to her father, berating him with her frustration. "I can't believe
you would do this to me!" she shouted. Then, turning
on her heels, she grabbed her leather Gucci bag and
disappeared into the elevators.

James sighed deeply. "I apologize for my daughter's
bad behavior. I know she's caused you both some grief
these past few months and I'm sorry for that, as well.
This will be good for Asia. It will give her something
else to focus on."

They both nodded in sympathy before shaking his
hand one last time.

The next morning Camryn rose early to run an er-
rand. When Darryl found his way to the lobby to meet
her, she was waving goodbye to James and Asia, who
were headed to Dubai to spend their holiday with the
royal family.

"Darryl?"

Kendrick calling his name pulled him back to the
moment. "Sounds like it worked out for all of you," he
was saying.

Darryl nodded.

"I'm not too sure about all that," Kenneth stated.

"What do you mean, sir?" Darryl questioned.

"I called James to extend my congratulations, as

well, after I talked to you and Camryn, and it seems that Asia ran into some problems going through Dubai customs."

"What happened?" Mason asked, his tone curious.

"There was an issue with her bringing in some contraband items. You know how stringent their laws are. Apparently Asia's carry-on bag was filled with inappropriate material."

"Inappropriate material? I don't understand," Darryl said.

"The girl had a year's supply of pornography in her bag. You can't do that in them Middle Eastern countries," Senior professed.

The men all burst out laughing.

"What in the world was she thinking?" Darryl said.

"Sounds like she wasn't," Senior interjected, tossing in his opinion.

Kenneth nodded. "James said she's being held in a Dubai jail while they investigate. He actually thought it was kind of funny. Made a joke about there being more in her Gucci bag than he even bargained for."

Darryl suddenly had a lightbulb moment. He stared into space as he reflected on the entirety of their trip. He shook his head, pulling his cell phone into his hands to dial into one of his banking apps. With confirmation in hand, he chuckled, his head waving from side to side.

"Excuse me a minute," he said, heading toward the other room.

"There he goes again," Guy teased.

Kendrick laughed. "Leave that woman alone! You're going to be married to her in a few minutes," he joked.

Darryl laughed with them, ignoring the comments

as he closed the room door behind him. He dialed Camryn's number.

"You didn't change your mind, did you?" Camryn answered.

"Not at all," the man responded.

"So what's up?" she asked.

"I was just thinking about when Asia and her father left the other morning. You were helping her with her bags when I came down."

"So?"

"Your father was just telling me that Asia ran into some problems in Dubai while she was going through customs."

There was a moment of pause before Camryn responded. "Really? I'm sorry to hear that. They didn't find a snake in her bag, did they?"

Darryl laughed. "Sounds like she had a lot of *snakes* in her bag."

"And you're telling me this because...?"

"I just thought you would want to know."

Camryn smiled. "Snakes will do that to you, most especially those big Mandingo-size serpents..."

"I'm sure. I can't wait to see you, Mrs. Boudreaux."

"I can't wait to see you, too," Camryn replied. "I'm looking forward to our honeymoon."

Darryl laughed. "Maybe we'll watch one of those sex tapes you purchased."

Camryn laughed with him. "I wish we could. But I gave them all to an acquaintance. It being Christmas and all."

Chapter 21

Camryn cuddled close to Darryl as they flipped through the pictures that had been taken at their wedding. The images made Camryn smile. She'd looked spectacular in her wedding gown and Darryl's silver-gray tuxedo had been quite flattering. All the women had worn deep burgundy-red gowns, and the men dark gray tuxedos. Against a background of flickering white lights, the ceremony had been one of the most memorable moments of her life.

She smiled as she nuzzled her face into his neck and pressed a kiss across his Adam's apple.

Darryl dropped the photo album, wrapping his arms around her. He clasped his fingers across the beginning bulge of her pregnant belly. Her stomach suddenly quickened, a muscle tightening beneath his palm.

"What was that?" Darryl flexed his shoulders with concern.

Camryn grinned. "That's your daughter kicking."

His smile widened as he pressed his hand tighter against her. Her muscle quivered a second time and he nodded. "My son is going to play ball."

Camryn laughed. "It's a girl, Darryl! I'm telling you now. Don't you be surprised when she gets here!"

"You're the one who's going to be surprised," he teased.

Lifting her lips to his, she kissed him sweetly. "Are you happy?"

"Abundantly happy!" Darryl exclaimed. "I can't think of anything I'd change about our life."

Camryn smiled. "I think I love you, Darryl," she said.

Darryl smiled. "I don't think, woman. I know I am truly yours!"

* * * * *

REQUEST YOUR FREE BOOKS!

2 FREE NOVELS PLUS 2 FREE GIFTS!

KIMANI™
ROMANCE

Love's ultimate destination!

KROM13R

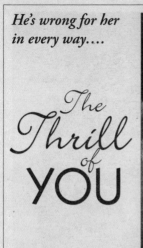